JENIKA SNOW

EVERNIGHT PUBLISHING ®

www.evernightpublishing.com

Copyright© 2016

Jenika Snow

Editor: Karyn White

Cover Artist: Sour Cherry Designs

Jacket Design: Jay Aheer

ISBN: 978-1-77339-004-8

JENIKA SNOW

DEDICATION

Thank you everyone for your support.

JENIKA SNOW

KINK'S WAY

The Brothers of Menace MC, 2

Jenika Snow

Copyright © 2014

Chapter One

Trash. Slut. Whore.

Those names had been thrown around so many times in Cookie's life that they blended together. She absorbed them, had believed in them for a very long time, but anymore she was just living from day to day. She could remember bits and pieces of her life as a little girl, not much, but enough that she remembered her mother sleeping with men right on the couch. Cookie would be watching blurry cartoons on a television that was on its last leg, hearing the gruesome sounds, but trying to act like she didn't know what was happening. Her father had been a bad man, done things she hadn't liked, and when he had left she had felt this relief. And then her mother had died when she was fifteen and she was left in the care of an aunt who didn't want her and an uncle who had been just as vile as her father. Her mother hadn't been anything special, and her death had just been another death that meant nothing to Cookie. To say Cookie's life had been a nightmare was an understatement, but she had prevailed, and fought every day to live. But of course when life started to look up the other shoe dropped, and her horrible life had gotten far worse.

She closed her eyes as the memories of her past, of a time when she was nothing more than a plaything, washed through her. When she opened her eyes again she was no longer in her past. Standing in front of the small sink and mirror at the bathroom in The Brothers of Menace clubhouse, Cookie forced herself to look at her reflection. She had her reddish hair pulled in a loose ponytail, but maybe having her hair away from her face wasn't the best idea. She could only see her flaws, the ones she tried to hide in her mind. Dark circles were under her light blue eyes, and a light smattering of freckles was across the bridge of her nose. She trailed her gaze lower until she was looking at her body, which was too thick for her comfort. Despite the feelings she had about her appearance, and the voices in her head from her mother telling her she was ugly and worthless, Cookie accepted who and what she was.

Bailey Marie Smith.

She hadn't called herself that name in a very long time, and honestly it didn't even feel like it was hers anymore. The name "Cookie" was something she had created as a little girl, because cookies were sweet and everyone wanted one. But the kind of attention Cookie had gotten was far from what she wanted.

Bracing her hands on the sink, she took a deep breath. She needed to get back out to the bar and serve the guys. There were a few regular girls that stayed with the club, and had been with them before The Brothers had taken Cookie and the rest of the girls from Denver in. There seemed to be so much going on around her that at times she felt as though she was pushing against water. The women Cookie had been with in Denver, the prostitutes who had been beaten by a pimp that was crazed and high, were trying to rebuild their lives. Instead of staying in a cabin that the club had set up for them, thinking about everything that had happened, and what could still happen, Cookie had decided to go back out into the world. She worked for the club, trying to keep herself busy, keep her mind occupied, and also thank the club in any small way she could for saving her life. Working at their club in River Run was what she could do now, and she hoped that they saw she was trying to move on. She wanted to keep her mind off of everything that had happened, and the best way to do that was to immerse herself in work.

She looked at the closed bathroom door, and could hear the music and male laughter on the other side. She had only been with The Brothers for the last couple of weeks, mainly helping behind the bar and occasionally cooking meals for them. But she usually just made sure they stayed drunk, and let Tatum, the clubhouse den mother of sorts, cook all the meals. She stared at herself in the mirror again, breathed out, and then washed her hands. No use in staying in the bathroom thinking about her crummy past.

But what would they think if they knew what really happened to her? The club members weren't saints in any sense, but then again being sold by her uncle to a pimp, and then becoming that man's whore, was probably not something they really cared much to know. She had been disgusted with herself for a very long time, but when a person had nothing to start with, and then suddenly was lavished with beautiful things and affection until they were drowning in it, it was hard for them not to latch onto that. And that was exactly what she had done with Morris. Even thinking his name made her stomach clench in disgust.

First she had been sold for nothing more than some eight balls of coke and a couple hundred dollars at the tender age of seventeen, and then she had been sold again by Morris when she turned twenty-one.

It was like some kind of sick joke played on her. She had lived the life of wealth with Morris, that disgusting sadist who had only been concerned about himself. And when he told her he wanted a younger, prettier version of her, he'd sold her to some rundown pimp that had beaten her and the handful of girls The Brothers of Menace had rescued. As bad as all of that had been, she knew it could have gotten worse. She hadn't been with the pimp who had abused them longer enough to be tricked out, so she was at least thankful for that part. But as sad as it all sounded, Cookie was glad that everything had happened the way it had. Because if she hadn't lived this life she wouldn't be free right now and actually planning on something more in her future than lying on her back with her legs spread and praying for death.

She opened the bathroom door, shut off the light, and put on her façade that showed that she was okay, and that she was this tough as nails bitch. She supposed in some ways that was accurate, but maybe that was because she had lived with that falseness her entire life, and it was like she was living the lie.

The main room where The Brothers of Menace hung out was this massive great room with timber detail, a beautiful loft above, and had been converted to have every amenity the guys needed to let loose. A pool table, huge bar that wrapped around one side of the wall, several pub style tables, and even a stripper pole had been added. She had seen a lot of shit growing up, most of it she would have preferred to forget, so seeing women wearing hardly anything, grinding on metal poles, and even sucking the bikers' cocks wasn't really a shock. Hell, she had done worse things than that—or had been made to do worse things than that in her time with Morris.

She stepped behind the bar and looked around the room. It was a Saturday night, and judging by the easiness and drama-free atmosphere, she would take a good guess that the guys were in a good mood. It wasn't like they didn't do this kind of stuff on a regular basis, but when they were stressed, or there was some kind of drama happening, Cookie could feel it in the air. It was like this dark, inky substance that covered her skin.

She saw the club members named Rock and Ruin over by the pool table, and the President of this MC, Lucien, sitting in front of the stripper pole. Lucien was watching one of the women shaking her ass in front of him, and then she bent down and grabbed her ankles, clearly giving him a shot of her crotch. Lucien reached out and smacked her on the ass, and the smile that spread across the club pussy's face told Cookie that she wanted Lucien to do more than that. A few of the other guys were at a table playing cards, and Cookie turned her attention away from all of it and focused on the liquor bottles lining the back of the bar. But there was one biker that she hadn't seen when looking around the room, a man that she had felt this weird charge of electricity move through her when she had first seen him all those weeks ago … Kink. He was the Vice President of The Brothers, and he always had this hard, unforgiving demeanor. It was one that frightened her and made her think of all the horrible men that had been in her life, simply because he looked like he was detached and didn't care about anything. But she knew that he was nothing like those bastards that had hurt her in the past. He may come off as cruel, not caring, and ready to beat someone's ass, but she had also heard that he had a daughter, one he loved very much. If someone could feel love, then they were not bad, and she could see that under that hard exterior, Kink was a good man, even if he was covered in tattoos and could kill a man with his bare hands.

She didn't know Kink from the next guy, and aside from a few conversations she had been involved in with some of the bikers, Malice being the main one, she kept to herself. It was better that way because once she was on her feet she wasn't about to stay in River Run. She didn't want to stay anywhere in fact. Cookie wanted to travel the country, not setting roots down in one specific place, and just enjoying being alive. There was nothing worse than someone forcing a person to do something, and Cookie would never let that happen to her again.

"Hey, sweet cheeks. Mind getting me a couple shots of Jack?"

She glanced at the man that stepped up to the bar. She knew him from the last few weeks she had been here, and knew that he was called Pierce and was a prospect. She had overheard the other girls that worked this place talk—and the bikers, too—that he got that name because he had some interesting piercings down below. She forced a smile and nodded, and without verbally responding grabbed two shot glasses, set them down in front of him, and poured Jack Daniels in them.

"Thanks, darlin'." He gave her a wink and a grin that she knew probably had most women spreading wide for him, and walked over to the pool table. Tuck and Malice were in the middle of a game, as were a few other prospects they had just recruited. She didn't mind the drinking, the wild atmosphere, or even the fact these guys liked their pot. She was just thankful that Lucien had let her work for him. Staying in that cabin day in and day out, seeing the girls who had gotten beaten the worst, and knowing that she could have been dead right now if things had gone differently, had her thankful for every little scrap she got.

Hearing something behind her, Cookie turned around. Pepper, one of the girls who worked at the clubhouse and slept around with the members, stepped behind the bar and was clearly looking for something. Tonight Pepper wore a very small black ruffled skirt, one that barely covered the cheeks of her ass when she bent over, and a white button-up blouse that was short enough that she had it tied right below her breasts. Her flat belly was on clear display, and the ring that was through her navel dangled and showed a little Playboy Bunny icon on the end.

"Hey, girl, have you seen that rock thing?" Pepper asked, bending over and rummaging through the bottom shelf.

"Rock thing?"

Pepper stood and looked at Cookie. "Yeah, that big ass piece of rock that you can stick a liquor bottle into and pour shots out of?"

Cookie nodded. "Ugh, yeah, actually I have." Aside from Tatum the girls didn't talk to her unless they had to. She didn't know if they saw her as some kind of competition, but compared to them Cookie was a damn blimp, less than attractive and was absolutely no competition in any way. She turned and grabbed the rock Pepper was referring to. It was a slab of granite with a spout coming off one end. Pierce had actually brought it in one day for a card game the guys were playing. Why they didn't just drink out of the bottles was beyond her, but maybe they wanted to class shit up and make it feel as though there had a bartender right there beside them. She lifted the thirty pound rock, and handed it over to Pepper. The woman struggled for a second when it was in her hands, and Cookie smiled internally. That thing was probably heavy as hell for a woman of Pepper's size. She trotted over to the card table on her heels, which could have been considered deadly weapons, and set the rock down beside Tuck. The scarred biker reached out and wrapped his thickly tattooed arm around Pepper and dragged her onto his lap. There was a lot of debauchery going on, but what was different from watching woman whore themselves out—which was still essentially what these women were doing at the clubhouse—was that the club pussy, as the guys called them, were actually doing this to settle down. She didn't understand it, didn't know what the thrill and temptation of being an "old lady" to these rough guys was, but to each his own and all of that bullshit.

Before Pepper could call her over, Cookie grabbed a bottle of whiskey and headed over to the table. Compared to all the women in this place Cookie was dressed like she was going out in a blizzard. Jeans and a t-shirt weren't considered overly dressed by most standards, but when the female population in this place was wearing latex and spandex that barely covered a nipple, Cookie looked like a nun. She set the bottle on the table, but kept her eyes downcast and her focus elsewhere. She did her job, and that was it. But the guys were already three sheets to the wind, so they didn't try to strike up a conversation.

Good.

And then right before she made it back to the bar the front doors opened, and in walked Kink. He looked pissed. He had a cut above his eye and a bruise forming on his cheek. He had gotten into a fight clearly, but if he had a few scrapes on him she could only imagine what the other guy looked like. She turned her attention away from him and quickly made her way to the bar.

"I need something to fucking drink, and make it strong as hell," Kink said loudly, and although she didn't look behind her she knew he was talking to her.

She turned and faced him, saw that he was looking at one of the girls grinding on the stripper pole, and knew before he had even started that he'd be fucking her tonight. He just had that look on his face that most of the guys in here got when they were about to screw someone. Cookie hadn't realized she had been staring at him until he turned and looked at her. God, how long had she been watching him? It hadn't felt like very long, but even one second was too long. For a moment she still couldn't pull her focus away from him. He had this faux hawk thing going on with his dark brown hair, and although most guys just looked ridiculous with a hairstyle like that, it actually made Kink look more dangerous and rugged for some reason. He stared at her with his blue eyes, ones that were cold, void of emotion, and if they could speak would probably tell her to do her fucking job.

"I'm sorry." She turned and closed her eyes, feeling like the biggest dumbass for even saying that out loud. She quickly got him a double shot of the strongest whiskey they had, the kind that she had heard the guys curse at when they finished throwing them back, and turned to set it down in front of him. But he was still watching her with that impenetrable gaze, and all she could do was stand there and stare at him right back. It was like his gaze had frozen her in place. She swallowed hard when he grabbed the shot glass and drank it without ever taking his eyes off of her. He slammed the glass back on the table, didn't even flinch after he swallowed, and she knew he was more than pissed. Rage ate him up.

"Give me another one," he said while still staring at her like this damn predator ready to attack his prey.

She refilled his glass and set the bottle down beside him.

He smirked, but it was just a tilt at the corner of his lips. "Smart girl," he said and tossed that drink back as well.

"Brother, where you been?" Ruin asked as he came up and stood beside Kink at the bar.

"Sam Adams," Ruin said and winked at her.

She grabbed the beer and tried not to listen to their conversation. But it was hard not to be drawn into the sound of Kink's deep, masculine voice, or the way it made this tingling sensation travel through her body. She couldn't explain it, couldn't even understand it herself, because it was a feeling she had never felt before. It frightened her, aroused her, and confused the hell out of her.

She didn't know how much time had passed with the two guys speaking behind her, while Cookie busied herself with wiping down the counter and liquor bottles, but then she heard Kink speaking again.

"Hey."

She looked over her shoulder, not expecting him to be talking to her, but he was. He stared at her, and she lowered her gaze to his thickly corded neck. She could see tattoos peeking out from underneath the collar of his shirt, and then she looked at his arms. God, they were so big and muscular, and the tattoos that lined his golden skin made him seem even more lethal.

"Get a good look," he said in a monotone voice.

She snapped her gaze up to his face, felt her cheeks heat from embarrassment because she had been blatantly checking him out, and then shook her head like an idiot. "I … I, well, I'm sorry." She didn't know what to say, and the stuttering made her feel even more juvenile. To be honest she had never been really sexually attracted to a man. With Morris it had been more of a security thing she felt. With Kink it was so very different. He was big and strong, and she knew he could handle his own. He could protect her with his strength, and then there was the fact he was so very attractive in a non-handsome way. It was like a roughness that called to the very feminine side of her.

She should have turned around when he ignored her, but she didn't. He didn't smile, didn't even respond when she apologized. It was like he had wanted to embarrass her, wanted to call her out so she was forced to face what she had just done. He finished off what had to be his fourth shot, turned, and then made his way toward the couch that Lucien was sitting on. Another woman came up to Kink and started grinding on him, and Cookie knew she needed to stop acting so foolish. A man like Kink was not the kind of guy she wanted to get involved with. But right before she turned her back on him she saw him look up at her as the woman was grinding her ass and pussy on his lap. He grinned, freaking grinned at her, like he found it amusing that she was humiliated watching what was happening. Maybe he smiled because he liked her watching what was being done to him, or smiled because he found it amusing that she couldn't stop staring. Either way Cookie forced herself to turn away and finish cleaning, because at least that would help her keep her mind off what she really wanted ... Kink.

Chapter Two

Kink brought the beer to his mouth, took a long pull from the bottle, and glanced at Malice. The other man was speaking to Tuck, and Kink felt pretty shitty since he had gotten all up in the man's business when he'd first brought his old lady to River Run from Fairview. Kink had his own shit going on, but that wasn't an excuse to take it out on a member of the club. Malice and Tuck clapped each other on the back, and moved away, but before Malice could move past Kink and over to the bar Kink called out. Malice stopped and faced him but didn't say anything. They might get things done in the club, and leave their personal drama outside, but it was time for Kink to make things right. He stood, took one more hit from his cigarette, and snubbed it out in the ashtray on the table. He straightened, looked the other man right in the eye, and just said what he needed to say. "Listen, man, about getting in your face about Adrianna when you first brought her back to the club—"

Malice took a step closer, cutting off Kink. They were matched in height and muscle mass, but even if Malice took a swing at Kink, he'd accept it. When Malice had brought the abused and scared Adrianna back to River Run from Fairview, Utah, Kink had been in a bad place. Not only did they have a handful of women they had brought back from Denver, ones that had been beaten by their pimp, but they had also brought back club pussy from the Fairview charter. Now they were deep with women that were in trouble, ones that needed rehabilitation from their pasts, and others that just needed out of Utah because of some fucking crazed cult that needed their dicks ripped off for messing with the club.

"Listen, I know that you got a lot on your plate with Callie and Sarah and shit, and despite you being totally off the mark, and crossing that line about Adrianna when we had the meeting, I understand that your head was elsewhere." Malice placed a hand on his shoulder. "Let's just move on, okay?"

Just hearing his ex old lady pissed him off. But he pushed it aside because that wasn't what needed to be said right now. Kink nodded. "Yeah, brother."

Malice nodded. "Let's just keep the anger and violence for the ones that deserve it."

Kink nodded. "Yeah, man, definitely."

Malice grinned. "Good, now I need to see my woman." He turned and left, and immediately Kink looked at Cookie. Since she had come into the club's life, he had wanted her, but he had kept his distance and put her from his mind. He had drowned himself in alcohol, pot, and easy club women, and he had never felt as dirty as he did now as he stared at her. But nothing could change what he had or hadn't done, and despite wanting her, Kink knew that he couldn't be with her, not in the way Malice was with Adrianna. Cookie was a damaged female, had probably lived a horrendous life, and him getting involved with her would mean bringing her into the dangers of the club as his woman. He didn't know her personal background, but he had a vivid imagination.

He looked at her again and forced himself to sit back down. The thing he didn't know was if she had been prostituting herself like the other women they brought back from Denver. He knew that some of the women hadn't gotten that deep into the "business" yet, so maybe she was one of them? But he wasn't meant to have a woman of any caliber in his life. Kink had done the old lady route, albeit for a short fucking time, but he had tried. And now he had a seventeen-year-old daughter to show for the few weeks of trying to be a good man and settle down. He loved Callie more than anything else, but recently he had found out her bitch of a mother had been trying to move out of state with his kid. That was also another reason he didn't need any women in his life permanently. He had too much shit going on right now, and he couldn't devote any kind of meaningful time or emotions to an old lady, especially one that could be damaged in a way that he couldn't bring her back.

Aside from this club and the members that he thought of as family, Kink had nothing else good in his life besides his little girl. Okay, so she wasn't so little anymore, even had some punk-ass boyfriend that he had heard about, but in his eyes she would always be his baby. Callie was the only light in the otherwise darkness that consumed him in the life he led. He'd protect her no matter what, make sure she didn't make the same mistakes he had, and also steer her away from bastards like him. He might have kept her in his life despite the fact he ran with an outlaw MC, and had done a lot of bad shit in his life, but that had been his choice. Not having a decent old man when he was growing up, Kink was not about to let Callie be fatherless.

He scrubbed his hand over his face and stared at the ceiling for a second, trying to get his shit in order. But he was stressed the fuck out because of Sarah and her bullshit of moving to California with her deadbeat boyfriend. Talking with her hadn't done shit, and her threats of leaving because she had full custody were a load of shit, too. He had a guy that worked with the club looking into it all, and Kink was pretty damn sure that the bitch had no legal standings to just up and leave the state. Besides, his guy was good, and Sarah didn't have shit to her name. If she wanted a fucking battle, he'd give her a war.

The woman that was grinding her cunt and ass on him was named Lolly, or Lilly, or something like that. He couldn't remember, and frankly didn't care. He just needed to get off. The bare-knuckle underground fights had done a little bit of good in getting his anger out. Not much, but he was hoping a good session of dirty sex would remedy that. They didn't call him Kink because it was a cute name. He was about to show this willing woman what he liked, and all the filthy damn things he wanted to do.

He leaned back on the couch, and looked over at Lucien when his President stood from beside him. Kink grabbed the woman that had been giving him a lap dance, pulled her close, and kissed her hard. He pulled back and focused on the tits that were currently being thrust in his face, and then leaned down to take a stiff nipple into his mouth. She had a ring pierced right through the tip, and he felt his cock stir slightly. Despite being in need of a hot, wet cunt to slip his dick into, this woman was just not doing it for him. System of a Down's "Lost in Hollywood" played overhead, and the club pussy continued to rub herself on him. But Kink's focus was on the woman behind the bar, the one that was trying to look like she was busy and unaffected. He could still see her glancing at him. He didn't want to make her feel uncomfortable, because he knew she had probably been through some horrid shit, but there was something about her that drew him in. Even with all the things he was going through in his life right now, he actually found a moment of peace in looking at her, which even to him sounded crazy as hell.

She wasn't skinny like the other girls that walked around here, the ones that were desperate to be claimed by a Brother. He honestly didn't know what the attraction to the lifestyle was for a woman. A Brother's life was far from ideal. It was dangerous, violent, and they tended to make a lot of enemies. The only Brother that was tied down was Malice, but Kink knew the other man didn't see his old lady or his kid as much as he wanted to. The club took a lot of time and effort to keep things running smoothly, and with Kink being the VP he had a lot on his plate. He stared at Cookie, watched as she bent over to get something out of the lower shelf, and felt like a sick fucking bastard for checking out her ass. The jeans she wore tightened around the big globes. He liked that she was curvy and that her body was made to take a man like Kink, but then he felt like a prick for wanting to do the things that he did, and for having the images of her naked and spread out before him crashing through his mind. He wasn't easy during sex, liked it rough and hard, and of course threw a little kink in there, but he knew she wouldn't be down for all that. Given what her life was probably like, and the kind of fucking *he* liked, he would scare the hell out of her. But she needed to be scared, because he was far from a good man, and a woman like Cookie needed a good man in her life. Hell, what the fuck did he know about what women wanted? All he knew was the ones he kept company with liked to get a big, stiff cock pounded into them.

"Come on, baby, how about you take me back to your room like last time?" The woman grinding on him spoke against his ear.

He pulled back and looked at her face. How sad was it he didn't even remember having her in his bed? The way she was moving over him, trying to entice him and get him hard, should have had his dick standing at attention. But he was barely semi-hard as it was, and he didn't know if it was because of all the shit that was going on with Sarah and Callie, or the fact he really wanted Cookie in his bed. He glanced at her again, saw that she was talking to Pierce, and felt this totally misplaced feeling move inside of him.

Jealousy. He felt jealous that Pierce was talking to her, and the way he was leaning over the bar and rubbing the pads of his fingers on the bar top and close to her hands told Kink the prospect was trying to get her to give it up. And then Cookie smiled at something Pierce said, and even from the distance and with the piss poor lighting he could see that Cookie's cheeks turned pink.

That pissed him off even further, and his jealousy roared up like some kind of feral animal. Kink pushed the stripper off of him and moved toward the bar. Cookie looked up at him and took a step back. Her eyes widened, and she glanced at Pierce, and then back at Kink. He knew his expression was probably pretty damn fierce, because he felt like slamming his fist into a man that would most likely be a member of this MC in the very near future.

Pierce turned and glanced at Kink over his shoulder, and then slowly rose to his full six and a half foot height and faced him. "What's up, man? You look ready to kick someone's ass."

He was, and that man was Pierce.

Kink stopped right in front of him, stared the other man right in the damn eyes, and tried to control his breathing. He shouldn't have been acting like a fool, but he and felt this anger the likes of which he had never felt before, and all because Pierce was hitting on a woman that wasn't even Kink's. "Yeah, I am ready to beat someone's ass." There couldn't have been any mistake that Kink was talking about Pierce, and when the other man flared his nostrils Kink knew he had picked up on the fact.

"What the fuck is the problem?" Pierce said, and the heat from his body came at Kink like a shot to the face.

"You're my problem, boy," Kink gritted out, knowing that the way he was acting was totally unjustifiable and misplaced, but unable to stop himself from acting on his raw emotions. They stared at each other, neither moving nor breathing, but their testosterone bouncing off between them.

"Hey, what in the fuck is going on here?" Lucien said and stepped up beside Kink. The scent of marijuana filled the small space that surrounded them.

"Ain't no fuckin' problem with me. The VP came up on me like I was pissing on his territory or something," Pierce said, and then his nostrils flared once more. He turned and glanced at what Kink assumed was Cookie. When he looked back at Kink there was a smirk on his face. "Oh, I see how it is."

"Do you now?" Kink said with barely restrained anger.

Pierce held up his hands. "I didn't know you called dibs. The barmaid is all yours, brother."

Before Kink could say anything in return Pierce moved past him and moved over to where Kink had just been sitting. The stripper took up residence right on Pierce's lap, and started grinding her shit like she hadn't just been propositioning him for some deep dicking.

"Kink, man, come talk with me," Lucien said.

Kink turned and looked at the President of the club. Lucien stared at him, inhaled deeply from his joint, and then slowly exhaled. The sweet smelling white cloud floated around them, and finally Kink nodded and scrubbed a hand over his face. He was fucking losing it. The stubble on his cheeks scraped along his palm, and the humiliation of what he had almost done filled him. He turned and stared at Cookie. She watched him with her eyes wide. The color was this startling blue that stood out against her pale skin and the light smattering of freckles along her cheeks and the bridge of her nose.

"Fucking hell," he gritted out.

She flinched after he spoke, and he felt like a motherfucker. He turned and stormed away, but sensed Lucien close behind. Instead of heading to his room that he had in the back, he turned and made his way toward the back hallway where a spare office was. Kink pushed the door open and turned to see Lucien step in behind him and shut the door.

"What the fuck was that back there, Kink?" Lucien said and leaned against the door. He crossed his big arms over his chest, and his leather cut stretched wide over his muscles.

"Shit." Kink shook his head and gritted his teeth. "I don't know." That was a lie, and when he lifted his gaze to Lucien he saw the expression on his President's face he knew that Lucien wasn't buying that bullshit line.

"How about you be straight with me, and don't tell me it is all because of Sarah and her crazy ass."

Kink shook his head. "It is mainly about Sarah and her bitch ass, but it's also about…" He stared at the door over Lucien's shoulder, and then shook his head again. "I don't know, man. I shouldn't have acted that way with Pierce, but I snapped. I have a lot of fucking brutal anger inside of me right now. I didn't want him hitting on Cookie when it is clear she isn't like the pussy that hangs at the clubhouse. In fact," he scrubbed his hand over his hair, "she shouldn't even be working here, Lucien."

His President didn't speak for a moment, but finally he exhaled and moved over to one of the busted ass chairs pushed against the wall. He gestured for Kink to take the other, and when they sat across from each other Kink leaned back. The chair squeaked from his weight, and the dust wafted from the old material and filled the room.

"I already talked to her about it, and she knew what happened in here even before she started." Lucien leaned back in his chair, too. "She is a tough girl." He grinned. "She's a tough Cookie, man, and insisted on being here. She needs to get her mind off shit, and who in the fuck am I to tell her otherwise?" Lucien stared at him with his eerie as hell grayish eyes, and Kink nodded.

"Yeah, I know, and I get that, but I still don't think having her see all this crap after what she has been through is such a great idea."

Lucien shrugged again. "Her call, and I'm okay with it. Besides, you didn't have a fucking problem when we voted that she was cool to be here."

He shook his head and stared at the ceiling. "Yeah, you're right. Let's move on." He didn't want to talk about Cookie anymore, and he sure as hell had no business caring what she did or didn't do. She was a grown ass woman and clearly knew what she wanted.

"So you don't want Cookie?"

He stared at Lucien, not knowing how to answer, because he sure as hell didn't know how to even put what he did feel into words. "I don't know what I want anymore, Lucien, but what I do know is that getting involved with a woman in a way that doesn't consist of me sticking my dick inside of her for more than a few hours is not what I need right now." He stared at Lucien, knowing his words were coarse and unjust, but he wasn't about to mince what he said. Lucien looked at him with this flat expression on his face.

"And a woman like Cookie sure as fuck doesn't need a man like me in her life."

Lucien was silent for a moment and then nodded. "I'll agree with you there. I think she's been through a lot of bad stuff, although I am not about to ask her if she wants to talk about it. I'm no therapist, and the last person a woman should be unloading her problems on." Lucien shifted on the chair. "Change of subject, brother."

Kink breathed out. "Yeah, I'd say that's a good fucking idea."

"But I don't think you'll like talking about Sarah either."

Kink shrugged "What the fuck does it matter? Aside from giving me Callie, she's ruined my life this far."

Lucien chuckled, but he knew it wasn't a jab at Kink's life. "You talk to that attorney I told you about?" Lucien asked.

"Yeah. The dude knows his custody laws."

Lucien grunted and nodded. "Yeah. Got his name from Molly actually."

That surprised Kink. "Yeah? Well, I'll have to thank her, because the lawyer told me Sarah doesn't have shit to stand on when it comes to trying to take Callie out of state."

"That's good. That's really fucking good actually."

Now it was Kink's turn to grunt. "Well, just because she isn't legally allowed to take my kid like that, doesn't mean she isn't a crazy bitch and won't try and leave anyway."

"You know the club has your back, and there isn't anyone that is going to take away what's yours," Lucien said with this hard bite in his voice. He stood, and Kink did the same.

"Thanks, brother." They clapped each other on the back, and Kink saw this serious look come over Lucien's face.

"You're my VP, and I have your back, but get it together, man. I need you level headed to keep this club running smoothly. I know you have a lot on your plate, and if you need time away to get it sorted just say the word."

Kink shook his head before Lucien finished. "I don't need time away. What I need is to get my daughter from that bitch, and everything will be good."

Lucien didn't respond right away. He took a step back and gave Kink a hard look. "You can bullshit the guys, even bullshit yourself, but don't lie to my fuckin' face."

Kink didn't know how to respond, because yeah, he was lying to Lucien, himself, and everyone else around him.

"Just get your shit together, yah?"

Kink slowly nodded, feeling his anger build once more. He loved Lucien like a brother, but that didn't mean he wanted to be talked to like a child.

Lucien turned to leave, but stopped right before he opened the door. He looked over his shoulder at Kink and said, "And quit acting like Cookie isn't anything to you, because no Brother nearly beats a prospect's ass because he was talking to a woman." Lucien didn't move, didn't change his blank expression. But that didn't mean he hadn't said those words with enough conviction and truth that Kink felt it all the way to his bones. "And don't start crap in the club again unless you are ready to claim Cookie as an old lady. Only then can you beat someone's ass over talking to her, you know that." There was a moment of silence that passed between them. "Because if you start this again and keep denying what you want, you and me will be throwing it down, got it?"

Kink didn't respond, just gritted his teeth and nodded. He knew he needed to get his act together, get his head straight, and he hoped his life could go back to the way it had been—without female drama that fucked with him. But Lucien was right.

Lucien left him alone in the office, and Kink sat back down on the chair. He breathed out and braced his elbows on his thighs, and stared at the rusted and dented file cabinet across from him. What he wanted to do was take Callie away from Sarah. Hell, he'd had enough talks with his daughter to know that Sarah ignored Callie, spent most of her time with her douche-bag boyfriend, and bitched at her for everything. He would have gotten full custody of his kid years ago, but his life was not healthy for a child. But then again look at what Callie had to put up with. As much as he wanted to just go over there, beat the boyfriend's fucking face in, and take Callie away from Sarah, he was going to play this one by the books. He didn't want his kid in an even harder situation, and he certainly didn't want to go to jail because of what he did.

He closed his eyes, feeling a lot older than his forty years. And then his thoughts turned to Cookie, and what Lucien had said. He wasn't ready for an old lady, and certainly not one that probably didn't trust men given her background. But he also couldn't lie and say that he didn't want Cookie, and that just the thought of another man even talking to her pissed him the hell off.

"Get your head together. Acting like this is dangerous for everyone."

And now he was talking to himself. He had seriously lost it, and he knew if he wasn't careful he'd leave a destructive path in his wake.

Chapter Three

Callie tossed back the third shot of the night, and hissed out from the burn. The alcohol was nasty as hell, but she didn't care. She was looking forward to the oblivion that the liquor would give her. She wanted to forget about Sarah, and how she was a shitty mother, and about Sarah's loser boyfriend. She didn't want to think about her mom trying to take her to California only because Dale got some shitty job with his buddies out there, and her mom was too much of a wimp to stand up to them. Callie's life was here in Colorado, and she didn't want to leave. She'd miss her dad, miss the mountains, and hell, she might even miss Robbie.

She glanced over at her boyfriend, saw him smoking a joint with some of his buddies, and curled her lip. Nah, she wouldn't miss him. He was a fun time for sure, well, when he wasn't being an inconsiderate asshole, but he allowed her the freedom and excitement she needed right now in her life. But he wasn't good enough that she was even going to think about giving it up to him, which he seemed to want her to do with increasing frequency lately, even trying to tell her that they should "seal the deal" before she moved.

She turned and grabbed a beer from the cooler on the ground beside her, and shook her head. God, to think she was wasting her time on him, on any of this. But it was a hell of a lot better than being in the same house with her mom. And then there was her dad, this badass biker that loved her unconditionally, but couldn't even take her away because his life wasn't "fit for a child". Well, he should have thought about that before he had knocked up a woman he had taken home from the bar. She saw Robbie stand and make his way over to her. He had a joint hanging between his lips and this cocky ass smile on his face.

"Hey girl, you want to get fucked up?" he said and pulled the joint from between his lips. He held it out to her.

"I'm already getting fucked up on my own. I don't need any pot to help that along."

His grin widened, and he brought the joint back to his mouth. He inhaled deeply and held her gaze with his own cold, black one.

That was the thing about Robbie: he thought he was God's gift to women, had this freaky wild side, and just didn't give a shit. Maybe that was why she had wanted him right away, because he could give her something aside from being bitched at by her mom on a daily basis, and living this dull existence. One would think having a biker father would have been an exciting lifestyle, but it was the opposite. Her dad kept her away from anything MC related. Although she knew the guys in The Brothers of Menace club, and even had a crush on one of them since she was a little girl, she never got to hang around the club members much even though she saw them like a second family. It sucked a lot, but she just hoped her dad was able to work something out so she didn't have to leave. Even if she couldn't live with him, she'd be eighteen next month, and no way in hell was she staying with Sarah after that. She'd move back to Colorado, and find a way to support herself.

Robbie moved closer to her until his chest pressed against hers, grabbed her behind the head, and leaned in low to press his lips against hers. She didn't know what he was doing at first, but when he blew the marijuana smoke from his mouth into hers, she pushed him back.

"You asshole." She coughed from the smoke, not because she wasn't used to it, but because he had taken her so off guard.

He grinned and went back to puffing on his joint. "Hey, I want you loose, baby." He moved toward her again and leaned in close so his mouth was by her ear this time. "Come on, Callie, how about you give me that cherry tonight?"

"God, you fucking pig." She pushed him away again. "Is that all you think about? And then trying to get me drunk, and what, take advantage of me?"

This hard look crossed his face. "You're one uptight cock-tease, and you're acting like a cunt right now."

She curled her hands into fists. "Fuck you, Robbie." The shots were really hitting her hard now, and with the smoke he had made her inhale, she was feeling pretty funky. She pushed past him and went to sit on the couch. But given the fact Robbie looked pissed as hell he didn't come over and apologize for being a dick. Instead he moved over to Laura Carlton, a slut from high school that gave it up to anyone that would buy her dinner. Callie narrowed her eyes when Robbie stopped right in front of Laura, leaned in low, and whispered something probably filthy in her ear.

That fucking asshole.

Laura smiled, looked at Robbie, and nodded. Yeah, the bitch was totally going to give it up to him tonight. Well fuck them both. Robbie looked over at her, smiled widely, but Callie gave him the middle finger and stood. Right before she turned her back on him she saw Robbie's grin fall. Good, she hoped the asshole realized she was the type of girl that would knee him in the balls if the time called for it. She snagged the bottle of cheap tequila off the counter and made her way outside. The backyard was small, with a bunch of junk lying in one corner. She didn't even really know the person throwing the party. It was more of a friend of a friend kind of thing. She took a seat on one of the busted up lawn chairs and took a swig of the foul tasting alcohol. The majority of the people here weren't even in high school anymore, and aside from Robbie, Laura, and a couple of other people that she really didn't hang out with, she was the odd man out at this party. She glanced at the bottle in her hand and grimaced. Her stomach roiled, and she set the bottle down. She was already drunk, and now high thanks to Robbie, and really just wanted to go home. She headed back inside, looked around for Robbie, and when she couldn't find him she headed over to one of his deadbeat friend playing cards in the corner.

"You seen Robbie?" Her voice slurred, and she cleared her throat and braced a hand on the table. God, the alcohol was really starting to come on strong now. A few of the guys glanced at each other, and although they hadn't said anything yet, she knew damn well what they were thinking. "What fucking bedroom is he in?"

One of the guys looked a little apprehensive, but he did point toward the back hallway. She looked over her shoulder, knowing what she was going to find, but not about to let it roll off her shoulders. She had never been the type of girl that just sat back and let people walk all over her, and maybe that was why she didn't have any friends that were girls. Hell, she hardly had any guy friends either, but she got along with them better than the bitches she had gone to school with. She turned and headed toward the lone bedroom in this piece of shit apartment, stopped at the closed door, and heard the moaning coming from the other side. Maybe she was sick for even contemplating seeing what was on the other side, or maybe she was a stupid ass for caring that Robbie was clearly fucking some slut. It wasn't like they had been going out for very long, a month really, but she had known deep down that he was not the right guy for her.

She twisted the handle and pushed the door open, and the sight in front of her really didn't shock Callie. Laura on her back, her legs spread as wide as they could go, and Robbie rutting around between them like he was an animal having a seizure. She didn't feel hurt, didn't feel jealousy, and in fact felt slightly sick at the sight. But what she did feel was hatred for Robbie, Laura, and most of all herself.

"I hope you liked nasty snatch, Robbie, because that's all you'll ever get."

He glanced over his shoulder at her, but before he could say anything she slammed the door and turned back to walk down the hallway. Everyone was staring at her, but she didn't care. "Get a good look, assholes," she muttered under her breath and stormed out of the apartment. Callie went down the cracked and chipped stone steps and started making her way down the street. She grabbed her phone, the numbers blurry, and cursed herself. She was so damn drunk, and no way was she going to call her dad or mom. She tried to call one of her guy friends, but all she got was the voicemail.

"Goddammit." She cursed aloud and saw a shifty looking bench sitting under a streetlamp. This neighborhood really wasn't really the best, but she needed to sit down because she was going to be sick otherwise. Once on the bench she looked at her phone again. It was already after midnight, and although her mom might still be up, the amount of bitching she would hear because she was drunk, and because Callie had woken her up, was not drama she wanted to deal with right now. Her father … yeah, not going to happen. He may be a hard ass, and frighten a lot of people—her included sometimes with his coarse attitude—but he had been more of a parent figure than anyone in her life. He wouldn't yell at her, wouldn't ground her or slap her around. What he would say was that he was disappointed in her, and that would hurt a lot worse than her mother striking her.

She stared at her phone and the numbers that ran together, and before she knew what she was doing or who she was calling from her contact list the phone was ringing and she was bringing it to her ear. God, she was getting drunker by the minute, or at least it felt like that. She leaned back on the bench, thinking she might have called Ian, another one of the guys she considered a friend. She needed to him to be up, because she needed a place to crash, and at least Ian's parents were usually passed out drunk, so they wouldn't have an issue with a girl spending the night. But no way in hell was she going home like this, and thank God she had told her mom she was saying over at the party.

"Hello?" The deep, slightly gritty voice that came through the phone was most definitely not a teenage boy's, but a grown ass man's.

Her heart started beating faster, and she pulled the phone away from her ear to look at the screen.

"Hello? Who the hell is this calling me this fucking late?" the man said again.

She stared at the screen, blinked a few times, and then saw the number and name that was brightly lit on the screen.

Lucien Silver.

He palms started to sweat, and her heart raced even faster. She had called the President of the Brothers of Menace MC, a man that was frightening, lethal, and hurt men with his bare hands when they crossed him. She had heard the rumors when she had been listening in on around her father's friends' conversations, and even then, knowing he crushed his enemies as easily as if they were gnats, she wanted him. He was also the same man she had been crushing on since she was twelve years old.

Oh God, she didn't know what to say even as she brought the phone back to her ear and stated to breathe heavier.

"Are you fucking kidding me?" he gritted out, his anger clearly coming through the receiver.

She heard sheets rustling, and then heard a woman speaking on the other end. God, he had been screwing someone and she had interrupted. She could hang up and pretend like this never happened, but he'd find out who had called him, and then all hell would break loose.

"You better fucking answer me right now, because I can find out who this is easier than you think."

Oh, she had no doubts about that. "I'm sorry, I didn't mean to—" She closed her eyes when a wave of nausea settled inside of her. She did not want to pass out on this street corner, and maybe it was a blessing that she had gotten Lucien. He'd help her, maybe even not tell her father about this. "I'm sorry I called you. I didn't mean to actually, but I need someone to come get me." Had he understood anything she had just said? It sounded like a mumble of words to her?

"*Christ*, is this Callie?"

Her pulse skyrocketed at hearing him say her name. She had to be sick in the head to have any kind of sexual attraction for a man that was in his forties, but she couldn't help it. "Yeah." She licked her dry lips. "It's me, and I swear to God I didn't mean to call you."

"Fucking hell, Callie, are you drunk?" He may have phrased it as a question, but she could tell in his voice that he knew she was. She was slurring her words for fuck's sake, and couldn't even see straight anymore.

"Can you come get me?" She heard him curse and then heard the sound of more rustling. "Please don't tell my dad."

"Fuck, Callie. Goddammit." He was stringing out curses now. "Where are you?"

She rattled off the address of where the party was, and told him she would be a few blocks down from there on a bench. She hoped he could find her with those shitty directions.

"Don't move, Callie. Do you understand me?"

"Yeah." She leaned back on the bench and felt her stomach tighten again.

"I mean it, don't you fucking move." He breathed out roughly. "Is there anyone with you right now?"

"No." God, her stomach felt like shit.

"Fucking hell, Callie. Okay, go somewhere that is discreet and wait for me, okay?"

She blinked back the dizziness, and nodded, but then realized he couldn't see her. "There isn't anyone around with me, Lucien, and this neighborhood is not good. I'm probably safest under this light, or if I try and walk back to the party."

God, did he understand any of that, because she sure didn't. The reality was even if he told her to go back to the party she didn't know if she would make it without either passing out on her damn face, or getting mugged.

"Dammit." He cursed again, and then once more, and then she heard a door open and close. The sound of a car starting came through the receiver, and she couldn't help but feel this wave of relief pass through her. "I'll be there as soon as I can, and if someone tries to mess with you I want you to fucking kick their ass, and worry later.

But I want to stay on the phone with you until then, okay?"

She nodded, but of course the sound of her phone beeping because the battery was dying came through. "Okay, but my battery is going to die."

"Of course it fucking is." He seemed to mumble under his breath. "Stay on the phone with me until it does, Callie."

She only managed to stay on the phone for another five minutes before her phone died. She shoved the now worthless electronic in her skirt pocket, which was a hell of a lot harder than it sounded, and leaned back on the bench. She stared at the house across the street. It was rundown, debilitated, and reminded her sometimes of how she felt on the inside. She didn't know how close Lucien was, but she hoped it was closer than the thirty minute hike her dad had to make. She just hoped Lucien didn't tell Kink, because if her dad found this out, or found out she had called the President of his MC, he would go fucking ballistic.

Chapter Four

Lucien should have called Kink right away when he got off the phone with her, but dammit he hadn't been thinking about anything else aside from getting to Callie and making sure she was okay. Kink was surely going to shit bricks when he found out his little girl was piss ass drunk and sitting alone at some fucking bus stop.

Lucien had just kicked the woman he had picked up at the club to fuck out of his house, thrown on a pair of jeans and a shirt, and gotten the hell out of there. Callie's mom lived about half an hour from River Run, and the address Callie gave him wasn't too far off from there. He turned onto the street where Callie should be seventeen minutes later. To say he had hauled ass to get to her was an understatement. When he scanned the sidewalks with his gaze and couldn't see any sign of her. But then this heavy knot formed in his gut, and that dread intensified when he saw that there were two thug looking guys sitting beside her on the bench. Anger the likes of which rivaled his fieriest emotion came forth like a damn tank.

He pulled the truck to stop hard enough that he heard the tires squeal on the pavement. The two guys looked over at him, but Lucien was already out of the truck and storming over to where Callie sat. She was leaning over the side of the bench, and he could see she had been sick. "You two, get the fuck out of here before I beat your assess," Lucien growled out, feeling like a beast was bursting forth from him at the thought that Callie was being hurt. They might have been trying to help for all he knew, but he wasn't a damn fool enough to think that they had been trying to do anything more than take advantage of her.

The guys stood, and these scowls covered their faces in identical expressions. One of them, the bigger of the two, pulled out a switchblade and pointed it at Lucien. "Old man, you better get out of here. This isn't your business, and people around here know when to keep driving."

"Dude, he's a fuckin' beast," the smaller of the two, and clearly the smarter one, muttered to his buddy. The guy with the blade cursed at his friend.

Lucien stopped, feeling a twinge of amusement move through him, but his rage was far more powerful. He had been in such a hurry that he hadn't even put his cut on, and clearly these boys didn't know who they were messing with. He didn't respond, just reached behind him and pulled out the gun he had tucked in the waistband at the small of his back right. He moved toward them and pointed it at them. The way their eyes widened and the clear fear that masked their expressions, pleased Lucien immensely. "How about this, you keep moving, mind your own fucking business, and I won't put a bullet in both of your dicks." He lowered the gun and pointed it at the crotch of the bigger guy that had spoken. "Because I don't think you two know who the fuck you're dealing with right now."

Both guys held their hands up in surrender and took off like the pussies they were. He tucked his gun in the back of his waistband once more, and quickly made his way toward Callie. Crouching in front of her, he pushed some of her dark hair away from her face and looked at her.

"Hey, you okay?"

She closed her eyes tightly and moaned. "No, but I feel better now that I don't have anything left in my stomach."

"Those motherfuckers didn't hurt you, did they?"

She shook her head. "No. They had just shown up a couple minutes before you came. They were trying to get me to go with them to their place."

Lucien curled his free hand into a tight fist and clenched his jaw hard enough he was surprised his teeth didn't crack. She slowly straightened, groaned out something about never drinking again, and he couldn't help but chuckle. "Honey, everyone says that when they feel like shit from getting drunk, but they always go back." He'd make sure she didn't though, because although he had been young once, and had been sicker than a damn dog more times than he could even count, he sure as hell didn't want her put in this situation ever again. "We need to tell your dad though, because if he finds out about this and it didn't come from one of us..." He shook his head and stared into her blue eyes. "Honey, he'll fuckin' lose it."

She shook her head, closed her eyes and groaned, and then slowly opened them again. "Please don't tell him. I don't think he needs anymore crap thrown his way. He's already stressed over my mom and the custody thing, and this will just piss him off more."

Yeah, she had a point, but this was the VP of the club, and a man Lucien considered as close as a brother. "Come on, let's just get you in the truck and we can worry about the rest of this later." Before she could stand he had her in his arms and was striding toward the passenger side door of his truck. Once he had her in the seat with the seatbelt over her, he reached in the back and rummaged around for a bag. He set it on her lap, pushed her hair away from her face again, and looked at her. Her eyes were closed, and she was pale and clammy looking. Yeah, she'd be feeling this in the morning. "If you feel like upchucking, do it in the bag."

She nodded and mumbled something, and clutched the bag closer. He moved back, saw the outfit she was wearing, and growled low in his throat. She opened her eyes and turned her head to look at him.

"Your mom let you out of the house dressed like a club whore?" He hadn't meant to be so crass with her, but why in the hell would Sarah let her wear a mini skirt and tank top that showed way too much of her chest?

Callie looked down at herself and then glanced at him with narrowed yes. "Did you seriously just compare my clothes with those skanks' that walk around your club?"

She was young, but had a mouth on her that rivaled the members of his MC.

"Besides, my clothes are fine, and my mom doesn't give a shit about what happens to me once I leave the house," she said while still staring at him. "She just likes giving my dad a hard time and being a mega bitch."

He chuckled at that. Lucien should get his ass in the car and take her to Kink's, but after yesterday and talking with the other man and the bullshit he had tried to pull, Kink had been on a binge of booze, fights at the barn, and taking women back to his room at the clubhouse. In fact, Lucien had seen Kink doing just that right before he left for his own place with an easy woman in tow. Taking her to Kink's was not an option, and no way in hell was he taking her back to the clubhouse where there was shit going down that a seventeen-year-old didn't need to see. "Kink would bust your ass if he saw his little girl like this."

She didn't respond right away, but finally licked her lips and exhaled roughly. "I'm not a little girl anymore, Lucien, and I don't think my dad needs to know about everything I do."

The way she said his name had this strange sensation moving through him, and he didn't much care for it.

"Can I just crash at your place tonight?"

He opened his mouth to tell her fuck no, but she surprised him by grabbing his hand and squeezing it in an almost pleading manner.

"*Please*, Lucien, just for tonight. I don't want my mom finding out I totally got this shitfaced, and have to hear her bitch, and I really don't have anywhere else to stay."

Even though he should have taken her to her mom's regardless of what she said, he knew how Sarah was.

"I know I shouldn't have been so irresponsible and reckless, and believe me it won't happen again, but I also know you, as well as my dad, have probably been in this situation more times than you can count." She slurred out her words and looked like she was fading fast.

"Fuck." He was cursing more in the last hour than he had in the past week, and that was saying something. "Kink is going to kill me." He shut the door and hurried around to the driver's side door. Once he was in and had the engine started, he headed to his place. This was a bad idea all around, but at the moment it seemed like the best, and only, choice he had.

He made it to his place in about half an hour, because now that he had Callie with him he didn't need to speed like the devil. He pulled his truck into his driveway, and cut the engine. The street he lived on was pretty quiet, and the house that he owned used to be his old man's until he'd passed away a year ago. Lucien looked over at Callie. She had passed out shortly after he had gotten on the road. As he skimmed over her, he realized she had changed a hell of a lot in the last year. It had been that long since he had seen her, but she wasn't the little girl that used to run around when the guys would get together. He hadn't meant to say she was dressed like a club whore, because in all honesty she wasn't. But that didn't mean he liked her wearing such revealing clothing.

He scrubbed a hand over his face, feeling like some sick pervert for even noticing her curves, and that she was showing too much skin. He cursed internally and opened his door before climbing out. Once he was on the passenger side and had the door open he lifted her easily. She mumbled something in her stupor, but actually curled into him. Despite her curves she was a tiny thing compared to him. She may have Kink's eye and hair color, and attitude to match, but she was built like her mom.

He carried her inside, and once he was in the spare bedroom, he laid her on the mattress. She smelled like booze, but no way was he about to get her out of her clothes that had vomit and alcohol on them. He took off her shoes and covered her with a blanket, and then he headed to the kitchen for a stiff drink. Setting his cell on the counter, and staring at it for a moment, he did contemplate calling Kink. But no doubt the brother was drunk and getting his dick wet. He grabbed a glass and a bottle of Crown, and poured himself a hefty amount. This wasn't the best idea he had ever had, and he knew that most likely it would backfire. He glanced over his shoulder and down the hallway, and this tightening in his chest intensified at the thought he had Kink's daughter in his spare room. Yeah, he was totally fucking screwed, and he knew that for a fact as he grabbed his cell, pocketed it, and took the bottle of whiskey to his room. He wasn't just pissed at himself for not telling Kink, but he was also pissed at himself because he was seeing Callie as a woman now, and that was wrong on every damn level.

She might be turning eighteen soon, but even if she was legal right now he wouldn't have touched her. He was too old for her, her father was like family to him, and getting involved with her would only mean a lot of blood would be spilled once Kink found out.

He shut his bedroom door and locked it, and then proceeded to drink away all the shit he had just got himself into.

****

As soon as Callie woke up she knew she had screwed up big time. She may have been drunk, but she remembered every damn thing. She pushed herself up on the small twin sized bed, and looked around. The feeling of nausea, dizziness, and an overall sense of feeling like shit washed through her. She also smelled like liquor and vomit, and humiliation filled her that Lucien had seen her like this. It had been a horrendous mistake to call him, but that had been what it was … a mistake. She moved so she was sitting on the edge of the bed, and waited until she was pretty sure she wouldn't throw up everywhere. She glanced around the room. Yeah, she was in Lucien's place, and not because the décor gave anything away. It was bikerish, if that made any sense. It was barren of anything that wasn't functional. It also smelled of him. It was a dark, slightly sweet and musky scent that she had always associated with him.

She needed to get out of here, because the last thing she wanted was to confront him sober, and have to explain what in the hell happened back there at the party. She stood, prayed there was a bathroom attached to this room, and cursed inwardly that of course there wasn't. She grabbed her phone that was still tucked in her pocket, and although she knew it had died, she hoped she could power it up long enough to try calling Ian, or another one of her guy friends. It powered up, but just as she was about to dial Ian's number the damn thing went dead.

She moved over to the door, listened for any sign of life on the other side, and only when it was silent did she open it. But as soon as she stepped out into the hallway the door directly in front her opened. And there stood Lucien, in nothing but a pair of jeans that weren't even buttoned. Beads of water dripped off his chest, and he ran a small towel over his short hair. He froze, as did she, and they stared at each other for a moment.

"You're up early." He lowered his arm, and all of his muscles contracted and flexed from the act.

God, he was a big guy, with muscles layered upon muscles, and this strength that came from him like a punch right to the face. She didn't know what time it was, but what she did know was that she needed to get out of here before she made an even bigger fool of herself. She lowered her gaze to the center of his chest, saw the massive tattoo of the patch for The Brothers of Menace, and swallowed roughly. She knew all the members had a patch tattoo somewhere on their body. Her father had one on his pectoral muscle, and she had seen a few of the other guys' ink that were in the club when they had been working on their bikes shirtless. But seeing Lucien's ink, that big, round tattoo that showed this rising phoenix, right in the center of his chest, had this heat filling her. She swallowed, licked her lips that had gotten so dry when she had seen him, and opened her mouth to say something … anything.

"Mornin'. You ready to go home? Call your old man?" he asked.

She nodded, but not to the latter. "I'm ready to go home, but calling my dad," she gave this awkward, nervous laugh. "I don't think that's going to happen." She cleared her throat and looked at the ground. "Can I use

your phone? I'll call one of my friends to come get me."
When he didn't respond she glanced up at him. He had
his brows knitted.

"What the fuck are you talking about? I'll take
you home. Just let me get a shirt on." He stared at her for
a moment and then turned and headed back in his room.
He was covered in tattoos, from his chest and arms, to ink
peeking out from under the waistband of his jeans.

She closed her eyes, leaned against the wall, and
told herself to get under control. She had enough to worry
about with the move to California, and her father, and she
sure as hell didn't need to worry about this attraction to a
man that would never see her as more than the kid of his
VP.

Chapter Five

One week later

The flames were hot as fuck, and so damn bright and high that it looked like they were touching the sky. Kink stood around with the rest of The Brothers of Menace MC, and although the police had made everyone leave the surrounding area where the bomb had gone off, they hadn't gone away too far. They needed to work this out, find out where the fucking church cult was located, and deliver some hardcore retaliation.

"I want these motherfuckers dead," Lucien ground out. "I want to get the Fairview charter out here, want to hunt down these bastards, and hurt them as badly as they hurt us." Lucien was pacing back and forth now, and running his hand through his short dark hair. "I want to get Malcolm in on this." He stopped and looked at each of them. "I want him to hack the fuck out of their website, find out where they are, and then we are going to go there and take down every last one of those pricks."

Kink scrubbed a hand over his face and exhaled. He looked up, watched as the flames and black smoke filled the sky, and knew that was the best route. They couldn't stand by and let some church cult come into their town and hurt the ones they loved. Just thinking about the cult that had given their Fairview charter issues because they had prostitutes working with them, and had pulled this stunt, meant war.

"What if the girls had been inside, or one of our men in the cabin?"

They all turned and stared at Malice. He had been at the site when everything went down, as had Pierce, who was sporting a nasty cut on his temple. Malice pulled Adrianna close to him, and leaned down to kiss her on the crown of the head. His old lady looked a little rattled, but she also had this hard look on her face. She was a survivor, that was for sure, but being so close to an explosion like that, right in the next building, would have had any of them scared shitless.

"I want blood for this. I want to see them pay," Malice gritted out.

"For sure, brother. We all want them to hurt," Kink said and turned away from Malice and his old lady.

"We need to put the club on lockdown," Lucien said, and they all grunted in agreement.

This was bad, and Kink had a feeling it was only going to get worse before it got better. If the cult started this on their own turf, Kink knew that they wouldn't stop until whatever point they were making was made. Hell, he didn't even know this cult, not really. He knew they had some kind of religious mindset that anything that they didn't approve of was wrong. Aside from the few flyers with information about their warped beliefs that were mysteriously dropped off at the clubhouse, he didn't knew what their ulterior motive was. Sure, they were fucked in the head, but going around hurting people they didn't even know, solely because they didn't agree with their practices was so twisted and demented that they needed to be put down.

"Call in your loved ones for the lockdown." Lucien looked over at Kink. "You have Callie this weekend?" He nodded. "Yeah. I planned on going to get her tomorrow evening, but I'm thinking of heading over there now, although Sarah will bitch for sure."

Lucien ran a hand over his jaw. "We need everyone at the clubhouse tonight. We don't know if these fuckers will strike again soon, so we need to keep everyone safe until they are taken down."

"Agreed." Fuck, he didn't want his kid in the middle of this, and although chances were that she would be safe since she was in another town, he wasn't about to risk Callie's life. Then again he'd have to sweet talk her mom since he'd be picking her up a day early. But Kink wasn't about to let that bitch walk all over him. He'd let her do it in the past because he didn't want Callie in the middle of their shit, but his daughter was nearly an adult in age, and even more so in maturity. Sarah would have to deal with it because they were in a dangerous situation right now.

They all headed away from the fire and back to the clubhouse. When he had heard about what had happened he'd come out with them. The women who stayed in the cabin that hadn't been bombed were safe at the club. He couldn't help but think about what would have happened if they had been home, and if the cult hadn't bombed the cabin the Brothers stayed in. But it didn't matter that they hadn't hurt any of their people, and although he was fucking thankful for it, that didn't mean The Brothers of Menace weren't going to take out as many of those fucking pricks as they could. This cult had messed with the wrong club, and they were about to realize that the hard way.

****

Cookie folded a blanket and set it on the spare bed. She had already been at the clubhouse when the rest of the girls had been brought in. There had been a lot of curses, some crying from the weaker and emotionally drained girls, and of course a lot of talk about the bloodshed The Brothers of Menace were going to deliver on the ones that had dared screwed with them—their words not hers. She grabbed a few more blankets and some sheets from the basket she had carried in. There were three cots that had been brought into this room alone and another three placed in the room beside it. There were pallets that were made up on the floor, because as far as she heard they were bringing in family of the MC because they were locking everyone down at the clubhouse.

After setting some spare linen on the cots and beds, she made her way to the next room, but stopped when she heard the front doors bang open. Lucien was the first one that walked in, followed by several of his other MC members. And then there was a young dark haired girl that looked a little annoyed and a lot uncomfortable as she followed Lucien and his men to the center of the room. Cookie's pulse increased as she stared at Kink who followed in behind her, and then it plummeted when she saw him pull the young woman aside and whisper something low to her. It wasn't until she overheard the girl say something followed by "dad" that she knew it was Kink's daughter. Cookie was getting worked up over nothing. But even if she wasn't his kid, that didn't mean Cookie had any right to be angry over a man that she had no right to want.

"Cookie." Lucien called out to her.

The young woman turned away from Kink, and she stared at the man that she had these powerful, but totally misplaced and unrealistic feelings for. She didn't even know his real name, yet she wanted him more than she had ever wanted anyone else. It didn't feel like the sick and twisted feelings she had with Morris, or the saccharine, yet uncomfortable, sensation when she had been with the only man that had ever made her feel wanted. She stared right at Kink, and he looked right back at her. Cookie snapped out of this haze, because people were probably staring at her in confusion. She moved over to Lucien.

"Round up the other women so I can give the lowdown on the shit going on."

She nodded and turned to gather the women that were scattered throughout two different back rooms.

Once everyone was back in the main room, and a few more people had come through the front doors. She saw Molly and Dakota, and even Stinger. She had heard around the club that Stinger was a member of The Grizzly MC, Molly's new man, and that Malice and he had gotten into it when Molly had first started being with the Grizzly member. She didn't know about all the drama that happened between them, because frankly she liked to stay away from that anymore. Cookie had dealt with enough of it to last her ten lifetimes, but of course she knew it would not be the end of drama in her life. It was like she was a magnet for the toxic shit.

Adrianna was standing beside Malice, and the big biker had his arm wrapped around her, but when he saw his son Dakota he pulled Adrianna toward the little boy. She glanced at Adrianna, and the woman was pressed tightly to Malice's other side. She could tell the woman wanted to be there, but she could also see the way Malice curled his fingers into her side, as if he thought maybe she'd move away from him. What would it feel like to have someone want her so badly they were afraid she'd leave their side? She only knew about someone wanting her because of her body, or because she could give them something for a few hours at a time. The one thing she was grateful for was that she hadn't been passed around, not like the other girls who stayed in the cabin with her.

She moved over to the bar and took a seat on one of the barstools. The ten or so girls that stayed in the cabin were sitting at the couple of tables situated around the main room. A young man and woman moved up to where Tuck sat, and he embraced both of them momentarily. They both had the same blond hair and blue eyes as the MC member, so she assumed they had to be his kids. It had only been a few hours since everything had gone down with the bombing of the guys' cabin, but she was surprised they had gathered this many people in that short amount of time. There were a few other people, an older woman and man that looked less than pleased to be there, but stood close to Lucien. Maybe they were his mom and dad? She looked over at Kink again, and her heart sped up when she saw he was watching her. He leaned against the far wall directly across from her, and although he was all the way on the other side of the cabin, she felt like he was right in front of her. That was how powerful his presence was to her.

"Okay, it isn't a secret why we called the lockdown, especially since this shit is plastered all over the fucking news," Lucien said in a weary, pissed off voice. He started pacing back and forth, and the expression on his face showed he was deep in thought. "Without getting into specifics, all of you were called in for your own protection. Someone is out to hurt the club, and presumably everyone we care about." He glanced around the room at everyone. "Until we get the threat under control, I need everyone to stay inside this clubhouse." There were murmurs throughout the room, but no one argued with the President. "Since Cookie has been working the club for a couple of weeks now, she can give everyone the layout if you're not familiar with it, and show you where you'll be sleeping."

"I can help, too," Molly said after Lucien spoke.

Lucien nodded. "Thanks, Molly." He looked around the room again. "Members, I need a meeting." He turned and headed toward the room the club guys used for their meetings. Rock, Ruin, Kink, Tuck, and Malice all headed into the room with Lucien, and they shut the door behind them. There was a moment of silence, and it felt like everyone was staring at her. She didn't know why Lucien had put her in charge of this. Tatum would have been better at it since she knew about these things, or even Molly since she had been with a member of The Brothers for years. Instead, Lucien had put her in the spotlight, and given her this responsibility that might not have seemed like a big deal to some. To her was huge.

"Um." She glanced at Tatum and then at Molly, but both women looked at her like she was the one in charge. Had Lucien done this to further help her in branching out? "Okay, if the girls from the cabin want to follow me I'll show you where you'll be staying, and then I can set everyone else up." She glanced at Tatum and saw the other woman smiling. This wasn't even that big of a deal, but in all honesty, to Cookie, it felt like she was making some kind of monumental decision.

After she had everyone set up in the rooms, some on the couches out in the main room, and even a few upstairs, she moved to the backroom. She was alone here, at least for a moment until it was time to cook something for everyone to eat. But she needed this small moment of reprieve. It wasn't about having to play hostess to everyone, not really. It was more about the fact there was this explosion, and their lives in jeopardy once again after only weeks of being thrust into the underworld. She felt like she was losing it.

Chapter Six

Kink sat around the table and listened to Lucien go over the details of getting in touch with their hacker. Malcolm was a college kid that was the son of the doctor they had working for the club. He was a smart little shit, knew his way around a computer like no one's business, and they were pretty confident that he could get into The Church of the Good and Only—also known as the motherfucking cult that messed with them. Malcolm was going to mole those bastards out.

There was a moment of silence that filled the space around the table. "Tuck, is Malcolm on board with this?"

Tuck nodded after Lucien spoke. "Yeah, spoke to the kid right after you called me from the fire. Malcolm took down all the info, and is going to work on it throughout the night."

"Was he able to check out their site while you had him on the phone?" Malice said through a low rumble.

They all could have lost a lot from that bombing, but Malice and Adrianna had been right in the thick of it. That meant a hell of a lot to their Sergeant at Arms.

"He said he should have something by tomorrow, but he can't guarantee anything so soon." Tuck leaned forward and braced his forearms on the table. "When I had him on the phone he said their site was locked down pretty tight, meaning they have someone who knows their firewall and protection shit when dealing with people trying to gather their personal information."

Lucien nodded after Tuck spoke. "In the meantime, I want Rock and Ruin to start surveying the town, poke around, and see if they are actually staying in River Run."

Rock and Ruin murmured their agreement.

"I can go to Steel Corner and speak with Jagger."

The Grizzly MC was a group of bikers that lived in Steel Corner, the next town over. Although the two clubs had worked together in the past, things had settled down over the last couple of months. They only spoke when they needed each other's help, or when The Brothers needed to use Steel Corner as a main gateway to their whorehouse located in another town. But with the bombing they had immediately shut down that house, canceled any set-ups they had with some high profile johns, and put everything on hold until this was taken care of.

"Good idea, Malice, but take Tuck with you. See what Jagger and his crew have to say, and if they have any info on any fanatics coming into their territory and rustling things up."

"On it," Ruin said. Although they hadn't heard anything from Jagger, the President of The Grizzlies, that didn't mean those cult pricks hadn't started shit on Grizzly territory.

"Kink, stay here and make sure everything stays together and the girls are all right," Lucien said and looked at him.

Kink nodded. Even though there was this heavy stuff that was hovering over the club, the threat of another attack, and not knowing where to find the ones that were fucking with them, all Kink could keep thinking about was Cookie. The guys started talking about others things club related, and Kink let his mind drift for a second. It was insane to be thinking of a woman he didn't even know, having these feelings toward her that put him in a foul fucking mood if a prospect even talked to her. But she was so fucking gorgeous, and her strength made her as tough as any biker he had ever met. He had no right to want her. The type of life she needed was soft, quiet, and without drama. His life was filled with all of that and more.

"If anyone comes up with anything report back right away."

Lucien's voice cut into his thoughts, and he pulled them away from Cookie. They all stood and headed out, but before Kink left Lucien called him back in.

"Come here, and close the door behind you."

Kink shut the door and faced Lucien. He already knew what the other man was going to say.

"How did Sarah take to you bringing Callie here a day early?"

Although the club always stood behind each other if a member needed that support, they never asked about personal business. It was an unspoken rule among them that they were always there, but that if the issue was too much of a burden they could talk about it. But never did a Brother willingly ask about the shit another member was going through. It was just the way they ran things in their club, and it had always worked out that way. But here was Lucien, the President of the club, asking what was up, and although it was supportive of Lucien to do so, it was also uncharacteristic.

"She took it how she takes everything else, I guess."

Lucien stared at him, but there was this weird expression on the other man's face, and Kink couldn't place why he was getting this weird vibe from him.

"Something else on your mind?" Lucien asked, and knitted his brows. He shifted in his seat, and Kink would have assumed Lucien was uncomfortable about something, but that couldn't be right. Lucien was tough as steel and didn't let anything get to him.

Kink rested his elbows on the scarred table and scrubbed both hands over his face. He had enough crap in his life right now that he was thinking there was something going on when there really wasn't. "No, I guess I'm just pretty fucking stressed." He saw Lucien nodded, but still the man was tense as hell. "Sarah bitched at first, but then she realized she'd have the fucking weekend to herself so didn't care. She was heading out with that little prick of a boyfriend of hers anyway, so Callie would have been by herself." He dropped his hands to the table, looked at Lucien and leaned back in his own seat. "Callie was acting like something was bothering her, though, and she didn't want to talk about it. I'm sure Sarah is just getting under her skin like usual."

Lucien didn't respond, and Kink stared at him, wondering what was going through his mind.

"Something on your mind?" he asked Lucien.

Lucien cleared his throat and shook his head. "I'm good. You hear anything back from the attorney?" Lucien shifted in his seat again and glanced at the doorway.

Kink knew something was definitely off with the President, but clearly he didn't want to talk about it. "I was supposed to meet with him to go over some things tomorrow morning, but I should postpone it since all of this shit is happening."

"No, don't put that on hold. You don't have a lot of time anyway. Besides, he'll come here, and you can talk with him in the meeting room and get things sorted out."

"Yeah, I'll give him a call. He seems like things should be favorable, but I've got this fucking dread in my gut, and it only got worse after this shit happened with the cult, and now the bombing. Besides, I want Callie to come live with me. She might be turning eighteen, but I think she needs to get away from Sarah and her toxic attitude. "

Lucien grunted, scratched his jaw, and then finally nodded. "Yeah, but we are going to take out those fuckers that did this, and you can let the beast out, man." Lucien grinned, and Kink couldn't help but do the same. "Okay, go see Callie. I have to go check on my mom and her husband, make sure they are holding up okay, and call Tilly."

"Your sister coming in?"

Lucien looked up at the ceiling, and his face took on this hard expression. "She's a stubborn girl, and was giving me a hard time about not missing class and having exams. She is just as hardheaded as I am."

"She should be good, though, safe I mean. She's several hours away, and the chances of those assholes linking you two is low."

Lucien nodded. "Yeah, I know, but still, it would have made me feel a hell of a lot better if I had her here in the protection of the clubhouse."

"I know, but she is tough. She gets that attitude from you." Kink grinned. "I better go check on Callie if we're done here."

Lucien nodded and stood. "Yeah, we're good. I just wanted to see how everything was going."

"It's going." Kink chuckled humorlessly and felt the weight that was on his shoulders push down even heavier.

They headed out together, and instantly Kink scanned the room. He saw Callie sitting over by Molly and Dakota, and moved over to his daughter to make sure she was settled. Once he realized she was okay, he headed toward the bar for a drink. He tossed back the shot that Tatum handed him. He tapped the bar, and she refilled the glass. Once he had that shot back, too, he turned and glanced around the main room. He couldn't find the woman he was looking for ... Cookie.

"She's in the back," Tatum said from behind him.

He looked over his shoulder. "What?" Of course he knew who the hell she was talking about, but he turned and faced her fully and kept his mouth shut.

Tatum cocked an eyebrow, as if she knew he was bullshitting her. "Really, Kink? You really going to play the 'I don't know what the hell you're talking about' card?" She refilled his glass for the third time, and he didn't waste time in drinking it. "Listen, I've been walking around here for the last couple of weeks watching the way you look at Cookie, and the way she looks at you. It's exhausting realizing you guys are trying to fight something like this."

"I don't think this is really your business, Tatum."

"No, it's not, you're right, but I can see a pain and distance in that girl's eyes when I look at her." Tatum leaned on the bar and stared him right in the eyes. "But then she looks at you and all this life moves across her face for a second, and I don't even think she realizes it."

Kink leaned back slightly but made sure to keep his expression neutral. "I don't have the time, energy, or lifestyle to take on an old lady, let alone one that probably hurts every single day from the life she has led."

"Honey, I'm not asking you to claim an old lady, but to show that girl what it means to be wanted."

Kink would have chuckled at the absurdity of what Tatum was suggesting. "Let me get this straight, you want me to sleep with her so she can feel good about herself?" That was a pretty fucked-up thing to even suggest.

"No, Kink, I want you to show her that you notice her, that someone wants her, and show her that it doesn't have to be wrong or bad to be with a man." She stared at him right in the eye. "She is scared in the worst possible way, and if showing her that she is wanted means being with her intimately, then so be it, but only if she wants that. I didn't say anything about fucking her, you damn pig. You're so damn crass sometimes." She turned away and shook her head as if she was disgusted with him. She gave out a few drinks to some of the people that came up to the bar, and then faced him again. "Talk to her, and let her know you've been watching her, and that you've *seen* her."

This was a bizarre fucking conversation, and one Kink didn't want to talk about anymore. "I have had a mother, Tatum, and don't need another one." He turned and stalked away, but not before he heard her mutter what a hard, stubborn ass he was. She might have been right about that, but he also wasn't the type to fucking woo a woman into his bed, and he sure as hell didn't talk out his feelings. He headed toward the back hallway and toward his room. He needed to sleep and forget about the crap going on around him, but just as he reached his room and had his hand on the doorknob, he stopped.

Who the hell was he kidding? Tatum was right. He did want Cookie. But it wasn't just for sex, although he wanted her bad enough that his fucking cock ached. There was just this strength inside of her, and every time he looked at her he felt this part of his hard exterior cracking. It was crazy shit given the fact he had hardly spoken to her. But maybe when something was good and right, and supposed to happen, time didn't matter? He turned and looked back down the hallway and toward the kitchen door where Tatum had said Cookie was. This was probably a bad idea, but he found himself walking away from his room, and right toward the woman that he wanted more than he had ever wanted a female before.

Chapter Seven

Cookie needed to get back out front. She had been sitting in the kitchen for far longer than she should have, and she knew Tatum was probably wondering what in the hell was up with her. Cookie didn't know, though, and that pissed her off. She had never been so confused in her life, and none of it made any sense to her. She shouldn't even want a man in her life. She should hate and feel disgusted with men given what she had been through. But she had never allowed that to define her. Pushing forward and thinking that one day something would change had allowed her to have hope. The sound of the kitchen door opening and closing sounded behind her.

"I'm sorry, Tatum. I know I was back here for a while. You ready to start cooking dinner?" she said and turned around, but it was Kink who stood by the now closed door. She swallowed, felt her pulse increase and her palms sweat, and hated the fact this seemed to be her reaction to him anymore.

"Hi." She hated that she didn't sound stronger in the voice department, but aside from the couple of times she had served him at the bar, and the clipped words he had given her, they really had never been in each other's company, and certainly not alone. It felt like the walls were closing in on her, and she wiped her hands on her jeans.

"I make you uncomfortable," he said bluntly, and moved closer. He had his hands shoved in the front pocket of his jeans, and his muscles bulged out. His biceps were so damn big they looked like they would burst right through his t-shirt and his cut. He stopped on the other side of the stainless steel table between them, and she gripped the edge and curled her hands around it.

"Yeah, you do." She wasn't going to lie, because there wasn't a point. "But I think I make you uncomfortable, too." She didn't know why she had said that, but the words had tumbled out of her on their own. She didn't regret saying them, though, because she did think she made him feel a bit off balanced at times, like right now.

He didn't respond but moved around the table and stood right beside her. He leaned against it, crossed his arms, and stared down at her. But Cookie wasn't about to move. Cookie had seen a lot of frightening men, and Kink might be one of the most intimidating ones she had ever met, but there was no fear in her. The longer he stared at her, the more she felt her arousal grow. She was wet between her thighs, and that was a feeling that she was not used to, this need to be with a man so urgently that it made no sense. She was so confused as to how a man just staring at her could make her feel this kind of lust. What was it about Kink that made her feel like she was about to dive down into this darkness … a pit of darkness that she craved? The scent of the alcohol came from him, surrounding her, but there was also the crisp, pungent aroma of his leather vest, and a hint of exhaust from his bike. It was a weird combination, and one that shouldn't be arousing whatsoever. But to Cookie it made her belly twist and turn, had her body heating to a point sweat beaded along the center of her breasts, and had her wishing that she could have the courage to just take what she wanted.

"What's your name?" he asked in that low, deep voice of his that actually had her toes curling.

He didn't even know her name. That had the high of being around him vanishing. "Cookie."

He shook his head slowly, and a small smile spread across his ruggedly handsome face. "I know that, darlin'. I meant what is your real name." He lifted a dark eyebrow and curled the corner of his mouth. "Surly your folks didn't name you after a dessert." He was teasing her, and although she didn't even want to think about the people that had brought her into this world, she found herself smiling in return.

"No, of course not." She swallowed. "It's Bailey Marie Smith." Her cheeks heated uncomfortably, and the smile faded from Kink's face.

"Bailey, like the liquor."

She licked her lips and took a step back when he moved one closer to her. "Yeah, my mom was probably drunk when she had me." She wasn't joking about that, and was thankful Kink didn't start laughing. Despite all the stuff happening in the last few weeks, wanting to be with him was the last thing she should even think about. He probably saw her as nothing more than this slut that had been sold to men and passed around like an ashtray. How she wanted to tell him it was far from the truth. She had been a virgin up until her uncle had sold her to Morris, despite the nasty touches from the men in her life who should have protected her. Even though she had stayed with Morris, that lowlife piece of shit for far too many years, and he had finally sold her, she hadn't been passed around like a piece of meat. The Brothers had saved her—all of those women, in fact—before it had gone down that road. But she kept her mouth shut. It wouldn't have made a difference anyway.

"You're too young to be in this kind of lifestyle."

She straightened her shoulders. "And what kind of lifestyle is that?"

He didn't speak for what felt like long, grueling minutes. "The hard, unforgiving kind, Bailey."

She swallowed roughly at the sound of hearing him say her real name. She had never thought she'd like hearing a man speak it, but yeah, she liked hearing Kink say it a lot. She shrugged, not knowing exactly how to respond to that.

"How old are you anyway? Twenty-three, twenty-four?" He took another step toward her.

"Twenty-one." She breathed out and realized she had nowhere else to go when the fridge stopped her retreat.

He stopped when he was only inches from her, and lowered his gaze down the length of her body. When he made the trek back up to her eyes, he held her stare with his own for a second. "Yeah, you're too damn young to be in this kind of fucking life. And you're really too young for me, Bailey."

"My name is Cookie." She said that on a breath, knowing it was a damn lie. She liked hearing him saying her real name, liked the way it made her feel, too.

"My name is Kink, but I think I'd like hearing you call me Logan." He lifted his arms and placed his hands on the refrigerator right by her head. "That's my real name, Bailey. Logan Roberts, but Kink has always been who I was." He lowered his gaze to her lips. A moment of silence passed between them. "Do I make you nervous because you're afraid of me and what I'll do, or because you're anticipating it?"

A visible shiver worked through her, and she slowly licked her lips. He watched the act, and she wondered if he saw how hard her nipples were. "Both." She was afraid of him, and not just because of the way he made her feel. This man was older than she was, probably close to twice her age even. But the way he carried himself, like he was not afraid of what the world held, made her realize that he could take so much from her. He probably wouldn't even realize he had left her behind when he was done.

"I shouldn't even be here, you know."

She didn't say anything to his statement.

"But there is something special about you, Bailey, something that makes me feel pretty fucking strange inside."

Yeah, she knew the feeling. "Maybe you shouldn't explore that then." Was she trying to push him away? It seemed like that, but now that he was right in front of her, and she was inhaling the same air as he was, there was this moment that her body was screaming at her to leave and not look back. This man could hurt her, but not in the physical way that she had experienced too many times already. He could hurt her heart.

"I should leave, but I'm not going to. In fact, I haven't wanted to be anywhere else in a long fucking time." He leaned in an inch closer, and she held her breath. "But do you want me to walk away from whatever it is we are doing here, Bailey?" He stared right in her eyes, and she wanted to look away from their intensity, but she couldn't.

The smart thing to say was to tell him that yes, starting something between them was so very wrong. He didn't live a good life, so wouldn't being together make an explosion of disastrous proportions? But as she opened her mouth to say that, something sparked inside of her. It was that little voice that she had tried to bury so deep it would never resurface. She had hidden it, and waited until it could never resurface again.

You've never had anything in your life worth fighting for. But you want Kink, want to feel something that makes you alive. Stop being afraid, take off the mask, and take what you want for the first time in your miserable life.

It was the voice of reason, of temptation and need, and it was the one she didn't let outside because it frightened her. She wanted to live, and she was now free, had the man she wanted right in front of her, and her fingers itched to bring him closer. She could hear her heart beating in her ears, feel the heavy *thump-thump* in her throat, and actually felt the wave and push of her blood through her veins. And like something possessed her, just took control of her and pushed away all of her trepidation, apprehension, and nervousness, she reached up, grabbed hold of the short hair at the base of his skull, and pulled him down toward her. To say this was not normal behavior for her was the understatement of the century, but it wasn't because she had witnessed a lot of nasty stuff in her lifetime. Maybe some would say she was sick in the head, damaged and broken over the things she had witnessed at home, or the things Morris made her to do him, but she always felt like she rose above that, didn't let it define who she was, and knew one day she would be able to be her own person.

She pressed her lips to his, and for a moment he was so damn tense and hard beneath her mouth. Maybe he was scared himself, or surprised by her boldness? Either way she was not going to stop until he told her to. Then she would let the reality of all of this settle in. Right now it felt good to have him pressed close to her, to feel his hardness against her softness. She wasn't short by any means, but even at five-foot-six Kink towered over her, and made her feel more feminine and fragile than she had ever felt.

He pulled back, breathed out heavily, but was still close enough that if she just leaned in that inch she could kiss him again. But he didn't bring his mouth back to hers, and instead speared his hand in her hair, pulled her head back so her neck was arched, and placed his lips hard on her neck. For several long seconds all he did was lick and nip at her throat. He ran his tongue up her flesh, circled it around her ear, and growled out roughly. "You smell so good, taste so fucking good." He went back to running his teeth up and down her neck, and then pressed the lower half of his body against her belly. He was hard for her, rock hard in fact, and he started grinding himself against her. "You see what you do to me? You see how hard I am, and all it took was this one kiss to make me nearly coming in my fucking jeans."

A small gasp left her, but she didn't push him away, and instead gripped his hair tighter, and pulled him in closer.

"But you've made me this hard before, Cookie. You've made me like damn steel, and all I had to do was look at you."

Another shiver worked its way through her body, and she grew wetter. God, she was so wet.

"You want me to touch you?" he whispered roughly against her ear. "You want me to touch your breasts, your pussy, or maybe that juicy ass of yours?"

She was breathing heavier, not sure how to respond, but knowing she wanted to tell him all the things she desired him to do to her.

"All you have to do is tell me where you want me to touch you, Cookie," he said low, heavy, and his warm breath teased her hair.

She didn't say anything, just lifted her hand, took hold of his that was beside her head, and lowered it to her breast. "Here," she said softly, and when he pulled back to look in her eyes, she pushed his hand even lower still. "And here," she said when he was now pressing between her thighs.

"Damn, baby, I can feel how wet you are for me." He pressed his hand a little harder against her.

She rested her head back on the fridge and forced herself to keep her eyes open. The way he rubbed his fingers against her had all the muscles inside of her contracting and releasing. "This is so…" She didn't know how to finish that sentence. It felt right, so right in fact, but it also felt rushed, unusual. The sensations moving through her were like nothing she'd ever experienced before. They frightened her, excited her, and made her want to latch onto them and not let go. But she also had to be realistic. A man like Kink, one that she knew got around in the club with the willing women, certainly wouldn't want her for more than a few hours.

But do you want more than a few hours with him, Bailey? Do you want to give your heart to a guy that lives this kind of lifestyle, and that wouldn't want more than what is between your thighs?

And that damn voice that had urged her to take control reared its ugly fucking head, and told her what was right in her face.

"You still with me, baby?"

She blinked back the haze that covered her vision and stared at Kink. He still had his hand between her legs, right on her pussy, but there was a moment where he looked worried about her reaction. She wasn't going to expect more than he was willing to give, because honestly she didn't want to have to find solace and peace with a man. She could do that on her own, planned on it even. That didn't mean she wasn't going to enjoy the life that was before her, and be the one that decided who she took into her bed.

"I'm here." She breathed out. "I'm right here, Kink."

He exhaled roughly, as if he had been holding in his breath, and leaned his forehead against hers.

"It's me, isn't it? I'm too coarse and pushing you too far, too fast?" He pulled back, but right when he was about to pull his hand away she gripped his wrist and kept him right where he was.

"It's not you, and I want this." She emphasized her point by grinding herself on him, and gasping out at the spark of pleasure that action produced.

"Yeah, you do, baby." He groaned and closed his eyes, and pressed his erection further against her.

"But aren't you curious about me, Kink?" Her words had him stilling. "You know about me, or at least have an assumption about my past." She didn't know why she was even bringing this up right now, but a part of her wanted him to know that she hadn't been passed around, and that she had not willingly subjecting herself to a life of paid sex.

He shook his head and leaned in close to kiss her softly. "Does it matter what happened in either of our pasts?" He murmured the words.

"It might," she said truthfully. If he knew the shit she had been through, he might change his mind in going through with this all.

For a second all he did was just stare at her, and then he finally shook his head slowly. "It doesn't matter, baby—"

"I didn't sell myself. I was forced into this life, made to be the…" God, she couldn't even force herself to say all the degrading things Morris had made her do. "I was made to do things to a man that thought he owned me. But I supposed he did since my uncle sold me off for some drugs."

He didn't respond right away, but she continued.

"And that was after my upbringing was something you'd hear about in the bathroom of a rundown truck stop…" She took a deep, steadying breath. "And it was just as filthy, Kink." This was the last thing she wanted to talk about right now, but she wanted Kink to know. "My mother screwed people in front of me, and when she died I was forced upon my aunt and uncle that didn't want me." She refused to cry. "And then there was Morris, the man I said owned me. He was a sadistic asshole, like to torment me because that was what he liked."

He went to remove his hand again, and the expression on his face was hard, angry, and filled with something dangerous.

"I'm not saying these things to disgust you, but I would understand if you were." She took a deep breath. "And when Morris was done playing with me, he sold me to that pimp that started beating on the woman that had willingly sold themselves." Her eyes began to water, and she hated that she was showing her weakness. Cookie had done a good job of acting indifferent to everything, but laying it all out to a man she really wanted, but one she didn't really know, was hard. And all for what? Because she wanted him to see her as something more than flesh that had been used up?

"Fucking hell, Cookie." He brushed away a tear that she hadn't known had fallen. When he went to pull away she reached out and grabbed his thick wrist.

"Please, I want you to touch me, to be the man *I* choose to be with." She was breathing heavily. Although she had opened up a part of herself she hadn't shown anyone aside from this man, she still wanted him desperately.

"Baby," he said gutturally. "How can I be with you after you say something like that?" He took his hand away, but didn't move back. Instead he cupped her face with his big, calloused hands, and stared into her eyes "You're breaking my fucking heart, Cookie." He spoke softly, but with so much meaning that she felt, for the first time in her life, that she was wanted and thought of for more than what she could provide.

"I don't want to break anyone's heart. I didn't tell you that for sympathy. I want you, Kink, more than I probably should, but regardless, I am choosing you." Her heart was beating so hard it actually hurt. "I'm not looking for anything more than just being with you."

"Cookie," he said as if he were in pain.

"I don't want to talk about my past anymore, because I've done my best to move on from that time in my life. I just want something that makes *me* feel good for once." She searched his face with her gaze, hoping he saw the truth behind her words. "I don't want anyone to feel sorry for me. I just want to live, Kink, and I want to start living by being with *you*." They stared at each other, and then as if they both moved into action at the same time, they pressed their mouths together.

The kiss was fierce, hard, and unforgiving. They pressed their tongues against the other, moving them together in an act that was erotic, and so sexually charged that every part of her body tingled in awareness. She had her hands in his hair, tugging at the strands, and trying to bring him closer. He growled and nipped at her lips, had his hands in her hair as well, and tilted her head back so he could deepen the kiss. She couldn't seem get close enough to him, and was pressing herself against him like she was trying to crawl into his body.

"I want you right now, baby," he murmured, and then opened his mouth and pressed his tongue deeper into her. For several seconds he fucked her with his lips and tongue, delved in and out, faster and harder, and groaned against her so fiercely she felt the vibrations all the way to her clit.

"Take me back to your room, Kink." She couldn't believe she was being so brash and forward with him. This was a first for her, but she wasn't backing down. Placing her hands on his chest, she felt his body heat pulse outward. The crisp, leather scent of his cut filled her nose. The feeling of his hard, bulging muscles under his smooth shirt felt so good under her palms. He slipped his hand down her leg, lifted it up and over his waist, and dipped low enough that he now pressed his cock against her pussy. But then the kitchen door banged open. Kink didn't move, and in fact kept kissing her, but she felt someone watching her, and heat flared to her face.

She had her hands flat on his pecs, and she pushed him back. He retreated an inch, and this cocky grin spread across his face when he looked at who stood at the doorway. Tatum watched them, her scowl fierce and her arms crossed over her chest.

"Kink, I said to *talk* to her, not," she waved her hand up and down toward them, "do whatever the hell it is you're doing with her back here."

"I'm sorry, Tatum." Cookie was so damn humiliated. She couldn't control herself long it seemed. She had nearly screwed Kink right here, in the kitchen of the clubhouse with people right on the other side of the wall.

"Honey, don't be sorry. When Kink sets his mind to something Superman couldn't even stop him from getting it." Tatum rolled her eyes and walked over to the stove. "But I could use some help preparing dinner for everyone. I think a nice home cooked meal will help ease people a little after everything that happened." Tatum turned her back on them to grab supplies.

Cookie tried to move past Kink, but he caged her in again, leaned in close to her ear, and said in a voice low enough only she could hear, "I want you tonight, Cookie. I want to make you bite your lip hard enough you cry out and bleed for me."

He was making her hot all over again, but no, she couldn't succumb. She wouldn't.

"Later tonight, baby, I want you to come to me." He leaned back and stared at her. "And when you come to my room, all ready and wet for me to take you, I'm going to make *you* come. Hard." And then he winked, grinned once more, and tuned to leave her alone in the kitchen. She was wet, needy, and stunned.

"Girl, you better be prepared for a whole lot of trouble getting involved with one of these boys," Tatum said and looked over her shoulder. But there wasn't any reprimanding on the woman's face. In fact, Tatum actually smiled.

"Are you telling me this is a bad idea?" Cookie was only half teasing, but she did respect what the older woman had to say. She had been involved with this lifestyle for years, and she knew her shit.

Tatum turned around and shook her head. "No, I'm not saying that at all. I'm saying that if you think this will only be a moment of getting it on with a bad boy, you might be surprised at the lengths a biker will go to claim a woman."

Now it was Cookie's turn to shake her head. "I don't need a boyfriend."

Tatum chuckled. "Honey, there is no such thing as a boyfriend in this lifestyle. If one of these guys wants you, like *really* wants you, than they will not stop until they have every part of you." Tatum stared at her for a few seconds. "And that's the truth, Cookie. Kink wants you, and it isn't going to be for a few hours in his bed, that you can guarantee."

Chapter Eight

The dinner had been nice, if noisy, but it was very family oriented. People were laughing and smiling despite the shit that had happened. And even though the members of the club tried to keep this easygoing attitude, more than likely to make things more comfortable for everyone, she could tell they were tense and on alert. They probably had so many violent things on their mind it would make the entire room dark with the cloud.

But they had finished dinner hours go, things were cleaned up, and everyone was settling in for the night. The clubhouse was a big lodge style cabin. With everyone crammed inside, there were people spread out all over—the couches, the chairs, and all of the rooms on the first and second level were taken. But now here she was, standing by the bar and staring at the hallway that Kink had just walked down. It was now quiet, aside from the low murmurs she picked up from the rooms closest to the bar, and the ones sleeping on the couches.

"You doing okay?" Tatum asked from beside her. The other woman had a stack of blankets in her arms and bags under her eyes.

Cookie nodded. "Just tired and overwhelmed."

"I know, hun. We all are." Tatum smiled. "I'm going to sleep in the same room with Callie, Molly, and Dakota, so if you need me you know where I'm at."

"Okay, and thanks. Get some rest."

Tatum nodded and turned to head upstairs. Cookie watched her disappear down the loft and then turned her attention back to the hallway. Kink's room was the last door down the long expanse, and her pulse increased at the thought of actually doing what he said and going to him. He had stared at her all through dinner, and even when the guys had been sitting around drinking he had watched her still. It was this connection she felt when their eyes met, and she felt kind of silly for feeling it. Even at twenty-one she was young, but she had lived a hard life and felt far older than that.

She dried the last dish, put it away, and set the dishrag on the counter. She was going to do it, push everything else away, and not take into account that Tatum had been warning her about the type of man Kink was. She knew who and what he was, because she had been watching him this whole time. But she didn't care about any of that, even if she should, and found herself moving away from the bar. Cookie walked down the hallway, and stopped right in front of Kink's bedroom door. Did he know that she'd cave and come to him like a hormonal teenager? She took a deep breath, lifted her hand to knock, but before she could bring her knuckles down on the wood, it opened and she stood face-to-face staring right at Kink.

"Hey, baby," he said low, in that husky voice that slid along her like he was actually reaching out and stroking her.

He was shirtless, and the patch tattoo that was inked on his pec stood out in stark contrast to his tanned, firm flesh. He didn't say anything else, and neither did she, but he did step back, opened the door wider, and curled the corner of his mouth up. She stepped inside, hearing nothing but her beating heart as she glanced around his room. It was pretty much barren aside from a bed and dresser, and of course some posters that showed half-naked women straddling motorcycles. Right above his bed and hanging on the wall was a giant flag of The Brothers of Menace patch logo. The heat of his body penetrated her back, and she closed her eyes and felt herself grow soft for him.

"Look at me, Cookie."

She slowly turned around and stared at him. "You want this?"

She nodded, not even hesitating. "I don't think I've wanted a man as much as I've wanted you." Honestly, the only thing she had ever wanted more than Kink was to live her life on her own, but choosing to be with Kink of her own free will was certainly something she was doing for herself.

They stared at each other for a moment, and then they clashed together in a tangle of limbs, hands, teeth, and lips. He held onto her hips and walked her backward until she was pressed to the wall, right beside his bed. It was a massive one at that, king sized, with rumpled sheets, and his clothing scattered on it. He smelled of fresh soap, and she lifted her hands and ran them over his damp flesh. The wall was made up of thick logs, and they scraped along her back unevenly, but that only seemed to inflame her desire even harder.

"I want this for myself." She was the one to murmur against his mouth now. She broke away from him and lifted her gaze so she was staring into his face. Kink used one hand to cup her cheek and moved his thumb back and forth over her bottom lip. "I don't care that this will probably only be for tonight, and that I'll just be another piece of ass to you."

He shook his head. "You're not just a piece of ass to me, but I don't think I can be the kind of man you need, baby." He looked down at her mouth. "But then again I don't think I can just walk away from you either." He cupped the other side of her face and slanted his mouth on hers. He was gentle, not forcing or rushing, but letting her know that he wanted her, of that she was sure.

Cookie gripped onto the loops of his jeans and pulled him forward so she could feel his erection against her belly again. "I want this, Kink. *God*, I want this so bad." She had never said those words, and it felt liberating and free to say them.

He slipped his tongue between her lips, and another guttural groan left him. And then she moved hers along his like he had done back in the kitchen. It was like her actions broke something inside of him. He kissed her deeper, more possessively, and she relinquished herself to him.

"My cock is so hard for you, baby."

"Make me yours tonight, Kink."

He leaned in again until their lips were brushing together in the softest of ways. "Baby, you're already mine." He placed his hands by her head on the wall and looked into her face. "You're not just club pussy to me, Cookie." He pushed her hair off her shoulder. "I want you for more than just a few hours, baby." He ran his tongue along her bottom lip, and then the top, and a surge pleasure moved through her. "You're safe with me."

She wrapped her arms around his neck and thrust her chest out so it pressed against his. Her breasts felt full, and her nipples ached. She wanted to be naked with him above her, thrusting deep into her body, and making her see nothing but the two of them together. She wanted to feel the heavy weight in his hands holding her down, keeping her stationary so he could devour her. Cookie grabbed his hair again and said in a more desperate voice, "Make me forget about everything that doesn't have to do with right now." She didn't need to ask him twice.

Kink gripped her ass and squeezed hard. He lifted her easily off the ground and claimed her mouth at the same time she wrapped her legs around his waist. He turned them around and immediately set her on the edge of the bed.

She stared up at him, and watched as he pushed down his jeans. He hadn't had them buttoned to begin with, and because he didn't wear a shirt, when he pushed his jeans down and took them off, he was totally nude. Kink took hold of his dick and started stroking himself as he watched her. He was already rock hard, and she swore as she stared at his erection, it grew harder right before her eyes.

"You keep staring at my cock like that and I'll come before I'm even balls deep in your pussy, baby."

Her breath hitched at his erotic words. Cookie didn't want to go slow, and she wasn't about to be timid either. She took of her shirt, and tossed it on the ground, and then reached behind and unlatched her bra. Her heart was pounding fast and hard, and never had she wanted something as much as she wanted him. She tossed her bra to the ground, and the movement had her breasts shaking.

Kink's abdomen had ripples and indentations of muscle, and that defined V that was like an arrow right down to his erection. Cookie probably stared at him a little longer than she should have, but she honestly couldn't help it. She looked down at his cock again, and watched as he moved his palm up and down his huge shaft. His focus was on her breasts, and she wanted to titillate him like he was doing to her. Cookie gripped her breasts and started squeezing the mounds.

"That's it, baby." He was breathing harder and stroking himself harder, faster. His muscles clenched and hardened. The man was built, and his dick was no exception, long, thick, and with a crown that was wider than the shaft. A fresh wave of moisture left her. She was wet, almost embarrassingly so, but she wasn't going to stop this.

"Take the pants off, baby," he said in that harsh, almost animalistic voice of his.

Letting go of her sensitive breasts, she slid her hands down her belly, and stopped at the button of her pants. Once it was undone and the zipper down, her arousal started to mix with apprehension.

"I should go slow with you, make love to you, Cookie," he said on a groan.

"If I wanted to be made love to I would have told you," she said as she breathed through her arousal. "I want you to claim me."

He made this low, guttural sound. "Push the pants off, Cookie." He lifted his gaze from her breasts, and looked at her face. "Let me see all of you."

She stood, pushed the pants down, and then did the same with her panties. She wasn't embarrassed of how she looked, even if she knew there was scarring from Morris's attentions. They were small, white raised lines, ones she had gotten when he beat her with his belt when she disappointed him, or when he was turned on. God, he beat her just for the hell of it sometimes. This was her body, her life, and she wasn't ashamed of it. It was that strength that made her a survivor. Cookie saw the way Kink scanned her body with his gaze, watched as he stopped on the few scars she had on her thighs and hips, but fortunately he didn't comment on them. He did, however, clench his jaw tight, and she was pretty sure she heard him growl low in his throat.

"I don't want to go there, and I don't want your mind there either," she said with determination.

He swallowed, closed his eyes, but nodded eventually. He stared at her for several seconds, and then in a low, deep and deadly voice, he said, "Place your feet flat on the bed, baby, and spread them wide." He slowly trailed his gaze up her body, stopped on her breasts for a suspended moment, and then looked at her face. "I want to eat your pussy out until you come all over my face. I want my lips covered in your cream, Cookie."

Her heart felt like it was going to burst right through her chest. She did as he asked, placed her feet on the bed and spread her legs wide enough that she felt her thigh muscles protest from the act. For several seconds he looked at her face, and then moved his gaze back down her body and right between her legs.

"Look at that, baby, all pink, wet, and needy for me." He took a step forward and then dropped to his knees in front of her. He placed his hands on her inner thighs, and he exerted a little bit of pressure, opening her up one more inch, and leaning in forward. His hot breath moved along her pussy, and her inner muscles clenched.

"Lay back for me, Cookie, and let me make you feel good."

Cookie didn't take her eyes off him as she slowly lay back on the bed. She curled her hands into the sheets and felt perspiration start to dot her body in anticipation. He rubbed his thumbs along her inner thighs, moving closer and closer until she felt him gently brush the edge of her pussy. The blood moved right below the surface of her skin, and she heated further. But he didn't put his mouth on her like she thought he would … like she desperately wanted him to do. Instead, he lifted her legs up, pressed them to her chest so she was obscenely opened for him, and lightly blew a stream of air along her body. A shiver worked through her. Closing her eyes and curling her hands into the sheets even harder, she tried to steady her breathing.

Cookie lifted her head and forced herself to look at him. His focus was right between her legs, and this fierce, look covered his face. "Goddamn, baby, I am going to tear your pussy up until you won't even be able to sit down without thinking of me."

"You have such a dirty mouth." She gasped out and let her head fall back against the bed.

He didn't respond, just used his thumbs to spread her even wider, and then placed his open mouth right on her pussy. Over and over he moved his tongue from her clit, flattened it all the way down her slit, and then moved it around her opening before pressing his tongue into her body. The sounds that left him vibrated against her clit, and it didn't take much for her orgasm to start to rise.

"Don't think, baby. Just let go for me." Kink started renewing his efforts. He licked and sucked, rubbed and nipped at her until she couldn't stop the shaking that soon took over her entire body. "Oh, yeah, baby. I fucking love seeing you like this." He muttered the words right on her clit, and that little bundle of nerves swelled even further. And right when she started to come he moved his hands lower to grip her flesh in a pleasure/agony filled action. A startled gasp left her, but it wasn't to stop him.

Her orgasm crashed through her like a strike of lightning, stealing her vision, her mind, and her very comprehension of what was happening. She might have cried out, but all she could hear was the blood rushing through her veins.

"You doing okay?" Kink said in between running his tongue along either side of her pussy lips. She opened her eyes, lifted her head, and watched as Kink pressed his hips into the mattress continuously. He was dry-humping the bed, so lost in his own haze that he couldn't even control himself, obviously.

"You want more, Bailey?" He curled his fingers into her flesh, and a gasp of pain and pleasure left her. "You want me to give you it until you think you can't take anymore?" It was like he spoke in riddles, but she found herself nodding, muttering incoherent things, because she couldn't even form a word. "Tell me, Bailey, tell me you want more." He sucked her clit into his mouth, and she opened her mouth on a silent cry.

"I want more." She breathed out that word, not even sure if he heard her.

"*Christ*, baby. I am so fucking hard for you that I could come right on this mattress, just soak the fucking sheets." He still had his hands around each of her thighs, clenching and unclenching her. He lifted his head and looked at her. "I want to be inside of you so damn badly."

"Then be inside of me." She panted, held onto the sheets, and silently begged him to just take her already. She swore the air cracked and popped with the energy that came from him. He moved up her body, grabbed her hair in a tight, unforgiving hold, and kissed her hard. She tasted herself on his lips and tongue, and groaned against him. She could feel his length against her, and felt the tip of his dick press against her opening. Even though she was soaked for him, she felt the wetness of his pre-cum from his cock on her inner thigh. He pumped against her, over and over again, but never hard enough to penetrate her. She should tell him to get a condom, that although she was clean, she still wanted to be safe. Besides, it seemed like the *right* thing to do, the *smart* thing. But she couldn't form the words, and grew lost and heated from his kiss.

"Bailey." He groaned her name, and held her tighter. "I just want to slip inside of you, feel your hot wetness envelop me." He moved his mouth over her cheek, along her jaw, and sucked at the shell of her ear. "Will you let me, baby? Just let me be with you without anything between us?" He panted against her ear, and she swore lights danced in front of her vision. "I'm clean, baby, and always used protection." He pumped harder and faster against her pussy, but still didn't penetrate her.

"I'll be careful, Bailey, pull out even, but I fucking *need* to be with you this way."

The smart part of her said this was a bad idea, that she should tell him to get a condom because that was the safe and smart thing to do, regardless of what he said. But God, she wanted this, too. She had an implant that prevented her from getting pregnant thanks to Morris, but she knew nothing of Kink's past, or how safe he had really been. He pulled back, and looking into his face showed her a truth and vulnerability, a need and a desperation, that she had never seen before.

"It's up to you, but you see what you do to me?" He kissed her ear, and took hold of her hand without moving away from her neck. He placed it between their bodies ... right on his dick. He was slick with her need and his pre-cum, and then she found herself nodding and begging him to put it in.

"I've always been safe, Cookie, always protected myself," he said again, seeming to murmur to himself.

"I want this. I trust you." And she did. God, did she ever. Maybe it was foolish, but she felt that trust deep in her bones.

He grunted, and while using his hand to force her to curl her fingers around this thick, huge length, he thrust forward. She felt where their bodies were connected, and a wave of arousal filled her.

"I'm so fucking hard for you, that if I'm not careful I'll come before I even get you off again." And then he thrust all of his length into her until his balls slapped her ass, and she was forced to bit her lip hard enough she felt the flesh open up. Blood filled her mouth, but she didn't care. In fact, she wanted more, a hell of a lot more.

Chapter Nine

Motherfucker. Kink closed his eyes and gritted his teeth. Cookie was so damn tight, hot, and wet for him. It was nearing painful just being inside of her, especially when she kept clenching and unclenching around his cock. It was taking a hell of a lot for him not to start thrusting into her like some kind of frantic, crazed beast. She clenched around him again and again, and he curled his hand in her hair even tighter. He had his other hand on her hip, keeping her right where he wanted her. This was *his* woman, whether she knew it or not, and whether he had verbally claimed her as his.

She. Was. His.

This wasn't even the best time to want an old lady, and he sure as hell didn't need one with all the shit happening right now, but he couldn't help himself. He had seen her when she first entered the club doors, trailing behind Lucien and looking scared shitless. He had wanted to protect her, but he had pushed those feelings away, telling himself that he didn't want a woman, and she didn't need a man like him in her life.

Well, it looked like his hard-won control was slipping when it concerned this woman. He was taking her for himself.

Trying to deny himself was pointless, because being inside of her felt like the most perfect fucking thing in the world. He pulled out slowly, just enough so that the head of his dick was lodged inside, and then thrust back in. Each pump and retreat was making it harder for him to keep this easy pace, not that he wanted to go slow. Her soft pleas for more, for him to claim her harder and faster, chipped away at his resistance.

"Please, Kink, more. God, I want more." She had her hands on his biceps now and curled her nails into his flesh. He started thrusting faster into her, feeling his flesh become slicked with sweat, and loving every fucking minute of it. He had never felt this way with a woman, never had this deep rooted need to mark her, claim her, and make it known she was his. It had always been about getting off, using the club girls because that was what they wanted, too, and because they wanted to get it on with a member.

"It is so fucking good." He looked at her face, feeling the need to just close his eyes and get lost in the feeling, but he couldn't. He wanted to watch the ecstasy cover her face when she came, and that would be real damn soon. "I could watch you all fucking night while I was buried balls deep inside of you. I could look at your face all day long and never get enough." The look of euphoria on her face, of her reddened cheeks and parted mouth, was like a visual orgasm all in itself.

"I'm so close again," she said breathlessly, like she couldn't get any air into her lungs.

Yeah, he knew she was, could feel her tight little pussy muscles clenching around his dick. He thrust into her hard enough that he heard their slicked skin slapping together. He fucking loved hearing that sound, and loved feeling his body connect with hers right before he pulled out of her and repeated the action all over again.

"Oh. God. I'm going to come again." She cried out, tilted her head back, and bit her lip.

Before she exploded around his cock he pulled out, grabbed the base of his cock, and started stroking himself while he stared at her spread pussy. He jerked himself off, looking at the tiny hole he had just been buried inside of, and trailed his gaze up her cleft, and stopped at her clit. "Touch yourself for me. Rub that little clit." He knew she'd be sensitive after coming, but he wanted this, and wanted to see her touching that pink, wet pussy of hers.

She moved her hand down her belly, and although she looked tired she did as he asked. His balls ached that she obeyed him so readily. This low sound left his throat. He watched as she circled the little nub, moved her finger back and forth over it, and made a small noise every time she did it. "You're mine, baby."

She didn't stop touching herself, and he loved watching her do this for him.

"I want you, Cookie, and I know you want me, too." He looked at her face, right into her eyes, and willed her to see what he was saying. "I want you as more than a piece of ass."

She licked her lips and nodded slowly. "I don't want this one night either, Kink, but anything more scares me."

Yeah, he could relate, but life right now was royally screwed up, and despite bringing her close to him, which was the wrong damn move, he wanted her by his side.

"Do you understand what that means?" He knew she did, but this had to be her decision.

She didn't answer right away, but then slowly nodded. "I think so." She never stopped rubbing herself, and he never stopped jerking off.

"It means you're mine, no one else's, Cookie, and that I claim you as my old lady."

"God." She gasped out and started rubbing herself faster.

"Say you're mine," he said almost demonically.

Sweat beaded along her forehead. "I want that, Kink, but I also want my own life. I want to experience things, not be stuck in one place, and being with a man scares me."

He could also understand that, especially with what she had gone through. "I still want you, and would never hold you back from anything."

She blinked slowly, her breath came out faster, and he knew she was about to come.

"Say you're mine, and we can take this one day at a time."

It took her a few seconds, but finally she whispered, "I'm yours, Kink." She tilted her head back and arched her neck.

He stroked himself faster, harder, and felt his balls swing from the force of his actions. His orgasm raced up his spine, down the length of his cock, and shot forward with so much force he had to brace a hand on the bed beside her head to keep stable. He came long and hard, and he watched in this haze of dirty pleasure as he covered the top of her mound with cum. His seed covered her trimmed, red hair on her pussy, her lower belly, which was curved just slightly, and her belly button. Just when he thought he was done coming, a wave of pleasure came forth again as he stared at her big, full breasts with the light pink nipples. When he finally collapsed beside her, he forced himself to keep his eyes open, and stared at her. She was still on her back, his seed covering her and making him feel this primal desire to rub it in. It was like she was his now, in the most basic of ways, but his nonetheless.

He rolled over onto his side, smoothed his finger between her breasts, and loved how the corners of her mouth lifted in a sleepy smile.

"That was … intense." She turned her head and cracked her eyes open. "But so totally worth pushing my insecurities and fears away." She rolled onto her side, and now was the one to smooth a finger between his eyes.

For a moment Kink was speechless and couldn't even move. He had never had a woman look at him the way she was, or touch him so gently like he was something more than a dick to ride on. It sounded so coarse even thinking about it, but that was the truth.

"Is it weird that I wish we could stay like this forever?" She chuckled, and went to shift away, but he wasn't about to have any of that. He wasn't about to let her get away, not when he was feeling pretty damn strong for her. He wrapped his arm around her waist, and pulled her closer so that she was half on him.

"It's not weird, baby." He leaned down and kissed her on the top of the head. "I'm not used to this either, and I'm sure there were be a hell of a lot of bumps along the way especially with this massive fuck-up happening to the club right now, but I'm not about to leave you behind."

She smoothed her hand along his chest, and he felt the light puffs of her breath move along his chest. "I should head back to my bed, well, my pallet." She chuckled softly, and went to move away from him, but he stopped her. What he loved was that she didn't even care that she was still covered in his cum. It was almost like she liked having it on her, and maybe that was fucked-up to some, but to him it was some pretty deep shit.

He pulled her closer, stopping her from moving away from him. "No, baby, stay here with me tonight." He was getting hard again, and all it took was the smell of her floral scented hair.

"People will start talking," she said in a sleepy tone, but relaxed against him.

"I don't care if people talk, but I can guarantee they won't." If anyone thought to open their mouth about them being together, or give him shit about anything, he'd beat their ass. They stayed silent for a moment, and he allowed himself to not think about all the crap going on in his life, and just enjoy holding her.

"Are you scared?" she asked softly several minutes later.

He didn't know if she meant because of everything going on with the club, or because of being with her, but he wasn't going to lie. "Yeah, baby, I am, but I'm not the type of man that backs down either." He answered truthfully, and meant it because being with her both exhilarated and scared the hell out of him.

****

"Can you speak English?" Kink asked, leaned back in his seat, and crossed his hands behind his head. He stared at the lawyer that was working on his custody battle with Sarah, and waited for the spindly little man to finish speaking. He looked like the stereotypical attorney: thin, wearing a designer suit, hair perfectly styled, and thin-rimmed glasses perched on his beak-like nose. But Kink didn't care what the man looked like as long as he made it so that bitch didn't take his kid.

"Well, since Callie will be eighteen in about a month, even if she did try to take her, the minor could leave of her own free will anyway—"

"I don't fucking care when she turns eighteen, or if she is only in California for a month. Sarah isn't going to take her to another state, that much I'll fucking make sure of."

The lawyer shook his head. "Mr. Roberts, your ex…" Sheldon, the attorney, looked down at his paperwork, like he was searching for the right term to call Sarah.

Manipulative bitch. Sadistic asshole. Unsympathetic wench.

Those were all names Kink had called Sarah to himself, or to his brothers, and although it probably wasn't the right thing to do, calling his daughter's mother those names, the truth was she was all those things and more. She used Callie against him, had her entire life, and those couple of weeks that he tried a relationship with her after he found out she was pregnant had been pure hell. It had been because of Sarah that he had stayed away from a relationship and claiming a woman as an old lady … until now that was. He hadn't talked to anyone aside from Cookie about wanting her as an old lady, and although he knew the other members would back him up, he also knew now was not the time to get into it with them. They had to talk to the hacker in a few, so he needed this problem with Sarah solved and behind him. He only had the weekend with Callie, per the custody agreement, but because of the lockdown he wasn't going to send Callie back. That would probably cause a whole new shit storm with Sarah.

"Just calling her my ex is sufficient." Kink lowered his arm back on the table and drummed his fingers on the table as he stared at Sheldon.

"You're ex doesn't have any legal right to take your daughter out of the state without speaking to a judge, and having you in agreement. Since you are in the picture, to put it in laymen's terms, she would have to go through a lengthy processing situation, in which her attorney would need to bring this up with the judge."

"She said she is having her lawyer look through it, but I don't know if she really is, or is just hopeful I'll back down. I know she can't afford to go through a big court hearing, so it's probably bullshit."

Sheldon nodded and started organizing the papers. "Well, I can start filing for a hearing right away, whereas we can bring the threats she has been telling you to the judge's attention, and the fact she is planning to flee to California without notifying anyone legally."

"You think that we can get this done quickly?" Kink asked and leaned forward to rest his arms on the table.

"Honestly?" Sheldon didn't wait for Kink to respond. "Things like this can take months, but I'm going to expedite it because of the situation with her trying to take the minor out of the state. All we can hope is that it gets pushed through quickly." He grabbed his briefcase, stood, and held his hand out to Kink.

Kink looked at the offered hand, exhaled, and grabbed it. He shook it, exerted pressure, and stared into the man's eyes. Sheldon winced but plastered on a smile and took his hand back. Kink stood, cracked his knuckles, and rolled his head on his neck.

"I'll let you know as soon as I hear anything." Sheldon went to move past him, but Kink reached out and placed a hand on his shoulder. Sheldon was tense, but glanced over at him and smiled. He looked nervous as hell.

"Thanks for helping me out with this," Kink said, and let go of his shoulder. "I know this is a lot of shit, and I'm pressuring you to get this done quickly, but that's my little girl in the other room."

"I understand, Mr. Roberts. I have a daughter, and if I was in your situation I'd be taking the same actions as you." Sheldon nodded, and Kink took a step back so the man could leave. For a few minutes he stayed in the meeting room, leaning against the table, and staring out the window into the main room. Lockdown had only been enforced for the last twelve hours, and he didn't know how long it would stay intact. They still had to find out where the cult was, take them down, and only then they would feel safe in letting their loved ones leave the safety of the club. He didn't even know how he was going to work this out with Sarah, because he was sure there would be serious problems. She may know about the whole lockdown routine from hanging around MCs—hell, she had even been unofficial club pussy, sleeping with several club members at one point in time—but she was still a selfish bitch.

He saw Callie sitting on the couch with a book in her hand. God, she had grown up so damn fast. She had already graduated high school a few months ago, and he wasn't ashamed to say he had gotten choked up seeing his little girl walking across the stage. The whole club had shown up to show their support. She was as much their family as she was his. He smiled as she read up on some college information he had all but forced her to get. She might not know what she wanted to do, or even if she wanted to go to college, but he at least wanted her to look at the information. He was pleased she wasn't giving him a hard time about it, too. He watched Lucien walk up to the couch, and something in the back of his mind stood up and took notice. Lucien sat in the seat across from Callie, and although neither spoke to each other, he noticed Callie glance up at Lucien with just her eyes. She shifted on the couch, and then Lucien leaned forward and braced his elbows on his thighs. Whatever he was saying to Callie had her cheeks turning red, had her nodding, and finally had her getting off the couch and leaving the main room. Lucien leaned back, scrubbed a hand over his face, and Kink saw the way the President of the club tightened his hands on his thighs.

Kink stood, about to go see what that was all about, but when he left the meeting room and headed toward Lucien, their hacker stepped through the front doors. All of the members moved forward, and everyone else was ushered into their rooms. Malcolm looked like he hadn't slept all night, judging by the dark circles under his eyes and the mussed clothing he wore. Kink glanced around the room and made sure everyone was gone. Cookie had still been sleeping when he got up, but it was early, and he had kept her up pretty late last night. That thought had him grinning and had his dick stiffening despite the fact they were about to get into club business. He put her out of his mind and focused on what was at hand right now. Stepping beside Lucien, he glanced at the other man. Lucien stared at him, and this strange expression crossed his face.

"I'm good, man." Lucien looked at Malcolm. "You got anything for us?"

Malcolm nodded. "Oh yeah, a lot of shit actually."

"Good." Lucien tipped his chin toward the meeting room. "Come on, boys, let's get the ball rolling and take down these motherfuckers."

Chapter Ten

"I was finally able to hack into the mainframe of the church's website, but they had a screen over the site."

"What the fuck is that?" Malice asked on a growl. He leaned forward and had a scowl on his face. This affected all of the men, but Malice's old lady, Adrianna, had been right there, and therefore the brother was even hungrier for blood.

Malcolm breathed out, clearly exhausted, and glanced around the rectangular, scarred table. "It basically just means that they have someone that knows their computer shit. They had malware on the site, which basically was meant to crash anyone's computer that was trying to break through their stronghold they had set up. I know my computer programs, and can get past the most fucked up firewalls. With a little bit of tweaking, I got past it, disabled it, and was able to put a tracker on their server location."

"And? Can you get to the fucking point, Malcolm? All this technology bullshit talk is giving me a headache," Kink said, not meaning to snap, but he wanted these bastards taken out already.

"Relax, Kink. Malcolm knows his shit. We're all stressed out, but we need to keep our heads together right now," Lucien said, and the President sounded a hell of a lot calmer than Kink was feeling.

He glanced at Lucien. The other man was leaning back in his seat with a cigarette in his mouth, his gaze right on Kink, and his expression patient. The thing with Lucien was he was a calculating biker. He was hard and dangerous when he needed to be, but was also a smart man. He waited, bided his time, and then struck like a fucking lightning bolt. They were all deadly and violent in their own right, but Lucien was something totally different. Kink knew that in order to run an MC, a man had to be a cold son-of-a-bitch, and Lucien was exactly that. He knew how to strike, and he knew how to take down their enemy.

Lucien exhaled, and a smoky cloud covered the space before him for a second before dissipating. "Malcolm, what did you find out?" Lucien said, and took one more hit before snubbing out the cigarette.

"Okay, so their IP address led back to their main base in Utah. It's registered to the same address they have located on their site, but after moving things around, and getting into a program they had hidden, I figured out that they aren't even operating from Utah."

"Okay, so where are they operating from?" Lucien asked in a low, deadly voice.

"The address I found was right here in River Run." The table grew cold and silent. "I tracked it down to a warehouse being rented out in the corner of town, right before the Willowcreek county line."

Kink sat back in his seat. He was surprised to a point, but he knew the cult had been operating in River Run for the last few weeks, but he didn't know they were running their operation right out of a building located in town. "You think they are trying to set up shop permanently?" Kink asked Lucien.

"I don't know. They are in town, obviously, but if they are actually renting out the old warehouse. It's been empty for the last year as no one is stupid enough to take on an investment like that," Lucien said. "But apparently someone is now, or at least temporarily. I have a feeling the cult might be trying to branch out, maybe trying to recruit right here in River Run, or even Steel Corner." Lucien took out his cell, looked at it, and set it on the table. "Malcolm, you get a name of the one leasing out the warehouse?"

Kink glanced at the kid.

"Yeah, hold up." He typed something up on his laptop. "The name is Beatrice Herving, but I think it is pretty safe to say if anyone has this kind of firewall and software protection on what is just supposed to be a church website, that is probably a false name."

Lucien nodded slowly. "Yeah, no doubt it is a smoke name." Lucien stared off for a second, and Kink grew itchy as hell. He wanted to react, but he wasn't going to go into this blind. They needed to get as much info as they could get on these fuckers.

"I need all the information on the warehouse, the occupants, dimensions, blueprints, and whatever the fuck you can gather through the computer. If you need resources, let us know, and we'll make sure you get it," Lucien said, and Malcolm nodded.

"It shouldn't take me but an hour or so to find out."

"Thanks, kid. Mind waiting outside?" Lucien said and tipped his chin toward the door. Malcolm nodded and gathered his things before leaving. Once the door was shut again Lucien looked around the table. "Rock, Ruin, did you find anything out surveying town?"

"Spoke to some of those junkies that hang around the titty bar," Rock said.

"Wasn't sure about how much they are legit in knowing their shit about what happens around here, but then they started talking about some church people hanging around the strip, and even some protesting that what was going on with the girls shaking their asses for money was wrong and immoral," Ruin said after he exhaled.

"How do we know it is the same motherfuckers that bombed the cabin?" Tuck asked, and there was a deadly tone in his voice.

"We don't, but I haven't heard that there have been any protesters spouting off their bullshit since these fuckers came here," Ruin answered, and the way he was drumming his fingers on the table had the two silver rings he wore clanking against the wood. "Let's be real. This is a small town, and despite the fact that a few residents don't care for the bars and strip clubs that have come up, everyone sticks to themselves. There hasn't been any kind of protesting like what has been happening since before that church shit happened."

There was a murmur of agreement.

"Other than a few of the old folks trying to close things down the legal way and behind a judge's door, it's pretty quiet. In fact I'm surprised this cult wouldn't keep a low profile knowing they were going to do that to our place," Ruin finished off.

"It doesn't matter anyway because when we find them we'll make them pray loud for mercy."

There was a chorus of murmured agreements.

"You end up talking to Jagger? I know you went to Steel Corner last night, but weren't gone too long, so I wasn't sure what the hell was up with that," Malice said, and he was furiously chewing on the end of a toothpick.

"They're in when we need them. Jagger said when we know the details to hit him up and his boys will be up with guns blazing."

Jagger was the President of The Grizzly MC, which was stationed in Steel Corner, the next town over. The clubs had helped each other over the last few months, and had gotten pretty tight with one another. Having them as back-up would be a lot of muscle.

"The Fairview chapter is also coming in, and should be here in the next few hours. I spoke with Marx, and he's bringing several of his guys," Lucien said and leaned back in his chair again. "With The Grizzlies, our boys from Utah, and us, I think we can take on these fuckers, but I want us to be smart about this."

"I'm not sweet talking with them, man," Rock said, and although the other man played it off like he was easygoing, the biker could be a cruel asshole.

"No one is talking about anything with them. Once we know if they are holed up in that warehouse, the layout of it all, and any other information we can get, we are going in to take them out, and worry about the consequences later." Lucien picked up his cell, looked at it again, and set it back down.

"What the fuck's going on with your phone?" Kink asked and pointed to the cell in question. "You've been eye-fucking that thing since you took it out of your cut."

Lucien gave him a nasty glare, but it wasn't threatening, just more annoyed. "I got a call early this morning." He stayed silent for a second, and then ran his hand over his short dark hair. "Cain called me. He is getting out tomorrow."

"Well fuck." It seemed everyone said that at the same time, and then they were clapping each other on the back. But the excitement that one of the Brothers was getting out of prison was short lived.

"This is, bad, bad timing for him to be getting out," Kink said.

Lucien nodded. "Yeah, I'm thrilled he is getting released, but right now we need to keep our head in the game. We don't need Cain getting into more shit when he just got out, and I know if he realizes what's going on, he'll want to join in with a gun in each hand."

"The man is one crazy fucker, but this club is his life, even more so after…" Tuck stopped speaking, and Kink looked at him. There was a hushed, uncomfortable silence that filled the room.

Cain had been locked up for the last nine years for attempted murder after he caught the sick motherfucker trying to rape his sixteen-year-old daughter. The only reason the asshole was even still alive was because a neighbor had called the cops, and they had come before Cain could finish him off.

"Well, if Cain wants in on something, ain't no one going to stop him," Tuck said, and they all agreed. "You know he has to be itching for a little action since being locked up that long, so let's hope we get this straightened out before he is released. I'd rather celebrate with him, than have Cain jumping in on this right away."

Kink leaned back in his seat, rubbed his face with his hands, and didn't think things could get even more complicated. Yeah, they needed all the manpower they could get, but they didn't want Cain getting implicated on this, especially since he would just be released.

"Well, let's deal with this one thing at a time, and take out these fuckers. Then we can focus on getting this club back to normal." Lucien sounded tense, and exhausted, but hell, they all felt that way.

It was only a half hour later since Malcolm left the meeting room, but he was knocking the door.

"Yeah?" Lucien called out, and Malcolm pushed the door open. He stood in the entryway, holding his laptop to his chest.

"I got the info you needed, even dug up an old floor plan of the warehouse, and found out a piece of information you will be pretty interested to know." Malcolm walked in when Lucien gestured him forward. He set the laptop down, and turned the screen so they could see it. "The lease was only on a monthly basis, so that shows that they aren't serious about staying here, not in that location at least." Malcolm then brought up all the information they needed. "And here is the floor plan. It's pretty self-explanatory with the entrances and exits here," Malcolm pointed to two areas on the floor plan. "But this is what I thought you guys would find really screwed up." Malcolm brought up another document.

Kink scanned the items that were printed on the screen. "Those are fucking ingredients for a bomb." Kink pulled the computer closer: C4, nitrogen fertilizer, and a whole slew of other harmless household items, but put systematically together could make a pretty big bomb.

Lucien pulled the computer back toward him, and Kink heard the sound of the computer edge cracking because Lucien held it so tight. He pushed it back toward Malcolm, and leaned back in the seat. He was clenching and unclenching his hand on the top of the table, and the sound of Lucien gritting his teeth came from him like a shot from a gun.

"And you can see from the date printed on these emails," Malcolm pulled up several emails. "The only way for them to have access to these types of material, mainly the C4, is they have to have some kind of connection. This isn't run of the mill stuff that they can pick up at their local garden supply store. But also they have the blueprints of the cabin on your club's property that took the hit."

Kink stared hard at Malcolm.

"And you were able to find all this out right now?" Rock asked.

Malcolm nodded. "Yeah, I mean I stayed up all night getting most of it, but the invoice of materials is what I was working on out there. It took time since they had buried it pretty hard, but there isn't anything on the internet I can't break through."

"And that's why we called on you, Malcolm," Lucien said. "You know your stuff. Now, can you give us minute? Maybe head to one of the back rooms and crash for a bit if you want?"

"Yeah, you look like shit, man," Malice said, but there was no amusement in the Sergeant at Arms' voice.

Once Malcolm left the meeting room, the guys went over the rest of the information Malcolm had given to them. The room grew tense, and long, grueling minutes passed by, ones that were filled with anger, violence, and the need to exact revenge.

Lucien kept tapping his finger on the table, and everyone focused their attention on him. "The evidence is pretty self explanatory," Lucien said through his teeth. "The dates on the receipts were only days before the bombing, and they even had a floor plan of the cabin on our property that got bombed." The anger in the room increased. "Tonight we go in, infiltrate their fucking cult asses, and take every last one of them down," Lucien said in a low, deadly and calculating voice. "Any objections?"

The room stayed silent.

"Good, now spend time with your loved ones, have something to drink to wind down, because as it is you all are about ready to bust. Come nightfall those bastards will find out what it means to mess with The Brothers of Menace."

****

Nightfall was just in a few hours, and the guys were spending time with their families, and preparing for heading out to the warehouse as soon as night was upon them. Lucien sat on the couch pressed against the wall and stared at his mom and her husband, who spoke with Molly. Malice and Adrianna were playing trucks with Dakota, and Lucien could see the love the hardened biker had for his old lady and his son. To think that all of this crap kept happening to them, their families put in danger, and for what? Lucien loved the MC, but sometimes he did think about all of the people he cared about being put in harm's way because of them.

Tuck was sitting on the other couch across the room with his son and daughter, and the other guys were relaxing and enjoying this moment of peace before all hell broke loose. Kink had gone to the back rooms with Cookie, and Lucien could only assume why the brother had wanted to have some alone time with his woman. Kink might not have outright claimed Cookie as his old lady to the club, but he'd have to be fucking blind—all the members in fact—not to see the man had it bad for the redhead. Even after he had the talk with him, one that seemed ages ago now, Kink had been acting different. It might only be a small, subtle change, but it was a change all the same. There was still this tightness to the other man, a dangerous anger that could very well tear the club in two. Hell, Kink had gotten into shit with two men, one of them Malice and the other Pierce, and all because he wasn't dealing with what was going on in his life. But Lucien couldn't really relate to what Kink was going through. He didn't have any kids, didn't have to deal with a crazy ex, and sure as hell didn't have a woman that was tying him in knots.

On the heels of that thought he glanced at Callie, knowing that it was wrong to even be looking at her. But he was not able to forget about the traitorous shit he had done behind Kink's back. He might not have touched her, wouldn't even think about it given she wasn't even eighteen yet, but he had thought about her in ways he shouldn't have. He still felt like he had betrayed Kink because he hadn't even told his VP about Callie being drunk, and Lucien taking her back to his house to sleep it off. Lucien might not have touched her, but fuck, any man would be livid knowing a grown ass man had kept something like that secret, and had a high school graduate sleeping in his spare bed.

Callie looked over at him, but he hoped she was still pissed from this morning. He had sat down, told her that it had been a big fucking mistake taking her to his house and keeping this from Kink. She may have nodded, maybe have said that eventually she'd tell her dad, but that she wanted to do it on her own terms, but he could tell she was uncomfortable. Hell, he was, too. He had to look into his VP's face, knowing what he had done was wrong, but still not say anything. Lucien knew that he should be the one to tell Kink, but when Callie had all but pleaded that she be the one, he had backed down. Lucien never backed down, but with Callie he was finding out that he could be a totally different man, and he wasn't sure how he felt about that. Callie pushed away from the wall she was leaning against, said something to Tuck's daughter, Lila, and made her way toward him.

"Fuck," he gritted out softly and glanced around the room. Anyone that could see would be able to tell there was something up between them, especially since Callie seemed so different around him now. Lucien could really go for a beer right now, but he wanted to keep a level head for tonight, and whatever Callie was about to say to him. If he was smart he'd avoid her, but if that didn't send up a bunch of red fucking flags to everyone, he didn't know what would. Also, he didn't *want* to avoid her, and that pissed him off even more. But he didn't get up, and instead he leaned back on the couch. She stopped beside him, but didn't say anything right away. Instead she glanced around, probably seeing if anyone else was watching this awkward exchange. Everyone was busy with other things, thank fuck, because he didn't need a confrontation right now.

"Hi," she said softly, and sat down on the edge of the couch.

He nodded and shifted so he could see her. He had known this young woman nearly her whole life, and had watched her grow up into the beautiful woman she was today, but that didn't give him a right to even think about wanting something with her even if she was older. Even if Callie had been ten years older, she was the daughter of a Brother of Menace member, and that meant she was off limits to any of the other guys.

"Can we talk?" she asked in this almost timid voice.

He didn't want her to feel uncomfortable around him, but things had definitely changed. Things were dangerous now, and not just because of everything going on with the club.

"What's up, Callie?" He grabbed a cigarette from inside of his cut, knowing he should quit, but feeling on edge because of tonight and everything that had happened thus far.

She glanced down at her hands in her lap. She was twisting them together furiously.

"You don't have to be nervous, Callie." He put the cigarette between his lips, lit the end, and leaned back on the couch, and stared at her.

"Well, you know I do, and I'm surprised you are able to stay as calm as you are." She looked at him and smiled, and it seemed awkward as hell. "So," she cleared her throat. "I said thank you, but I want you to know I really appreciate all you did for me in bailing me out, and letting me be the one to tell my dad."

"You're Kink's daughter and a member of this club family, Callie. Any member of this club would have done the same." He turned his head and exhaled. "But he needs to know, Callie. When do you plan on telling him?"

She shrugged but didn't respond right away.

"He needs to know, Callie, because it's not right. I agreed to let you be the one because you asked, but if he isn't told I'll do it." He sat there, staring at her and seeing that she was growing increasingly uncomfortable by the way she was fidgeting. He didn't know how to put her at ease, though. The truth was he felt awkward as hell over all of this, and guilty on top of that.

"I know, Lucien, but right now isn't the best time. I'm sure you'd agree."

He nodded.

She looked at him again, shifted on the couch so she was facing him fully, and exhaled loudly. "Well, that was all. I just wanted to say thank you again. But once this is all said and done I'll tell him." Lucien inhaled, turned his head to exhale again, but kept his gaze on Callie. "Do me a favor."

She nodded slowly. "Okay."

He took one more hit, and then turned to snub the cigarette out in the ashtray sitting on the table beside him. He stared at her for a prolonged moment and then said, "Don't ever put yourself in that position again, Callie." He leaned forward, so close that he could feel her body heat, and practically smell the nervousness that poured out of her. "You're a beautiful, smart young woman, Callie, and you knew better than to get involved in shit like that. You could have been raped or killed, do you understand?"

She nodded slowly. "I know. I was having a bad night, and I know it wasn't an excuse, but it was how I dealt with it. I'm so thankful I have someone like you in my life." She reached out and placed a hand on his. He tensed at the touch and pulled his hand away quickly. She cleared her throat and looked nervous again. "I'm sorry."

He stared into her eyes, ones that were the exact same shade of blue as Kink's, and cursed internally. "Just don't fucking do it again."

She nodded again, her eyes wide, frightened almost.

"I just don't want to see you hurt, Callie, because if someone fucked with you…" He held her gaze with his own for several long seconds. "…I'd kill them." He said it deadly still. "Because you and I both know that if someone hurt you, this whole fucking club would draw blood because of it." He heard her swallow, but he needed to get away from her, because his emotions were raw right now. "Be careful from now on." He got up, headed toward his room, and grabbed a club girl that passed him in the hallway. Right now he needed a willing woman to help get this anger, frustration, and self-loathing out of him. Right now he needed a good, raw, hate fuck, and this club woman that was already rubbing her big, fake tits on him, was going to help him with that.

Chapter Eleven

Here Cookie was, sprawled out in Kink's bed, her legs spread, and his massive shoulders wedged between them. He had his hands on her thighs, his mouth on her pussy, and was sucking the hell out of her. She loved the little growly sounds he made, like he couldn't get enough of the taste of her. Some might think it was strange that she was so comfortable with Kink after only just getting involved with him, and after the crap she had endured during her life, but she grasped onto this feeling of completeness.

"Come on, baby, give me one more while I have my face buried between your pretty thighs."

And then she was moaning out in pleasure. When the second orgasm faded Cookie breathed out. She couldn't catch her breath, couldn't even concentrate as she tried to get her bearings.

"Tell me, Bailey."

She loved that he interchanged the names he called her.

"Tell me you want me to take you." The thing about Kink was that he was so very dominant, so alpha, that she couldn't help but surrender her body to him. He never let her down, always gave her more than she could handle, and she found herself begging for more. He murmured against her sensitive flesh again, and she sighed.

"I want you any way you'll give it to me, Kink."

He rested his head on her inner thigh, his warm breath teasing her folds. She wanted, no, *needed* to feel him inside of her.

He settled his body on top of hers and placed his hand on the back of her neck, bringing her head closer. Their lips were inches apart now, so close that it was maddening how much she wanted him to kiss her. She could see the glistening wetness on his lips, and loved that his mouth was swollen and glossy because he had been pleasuring her.

"Everything about you makes me so fucking hot I can't even breathe, baby." He ran his lips lightly across hers, not really kissing her, but tempting her all the same. He pulled back slightly, and she ran her tongue along her bottom lip, tasting herself. Cookie wanted so much more from him.

"All I have to do is think about you and my dick gets rock-fucking-hard." He ran his tongue along her top lip. "Nothing helps ease the ache."

Although she knew he was leaving tonight for club business, and although he didn't go into details with her about it, she knew he was going to exact revenge on the church that had hurt everyone. She was scared for him and wanted to spend time with him, because for all she knew he could die tonight. But she wasn't going to bring up why she was upset, or that she was so frightened for him.

She trembled as he spoke softly. He replaced his lips with his tongue and ran it across her bottom lip now. She closed her eyes and absorbed the sensations.

"You smell so damn good, taste so fucking good." He ran his fingers down her side. "Your hesitation and desire are like a drug to me, Cookie, like a high I can't live without." He pressed his mouth gently against hers before moving it to the shell of her ear. A moment of silence passed, and then he whispered, "And your pussy is the sweetest thing I've ever tasted. You're so soft down there, warm and wet, and so damn pink." He groaned out the last word.

Her blood pressure spiked, and a flush spread throughout her whole body. Her arousal slowly trickled out of her pussy and made a trail down the crease of her ass. She didn't have time to feel embarrassment over the latter, because Kink slipped his fingers between her legs and stroked her until her legs shook on their own.

He growled in her ear. "If not for my self-control I'd be fucking you right now, hard and fast, and listening to you scream my name because I'm making you feel so damn good." He slipped a thick finger into her and slowly pumped it in and out. "But I want to savor this, bring you as much pleasure as you're bringing me." He moved his mouth to the pulse point at her throat while he continued to fuck her with his finger. "You're so wet for me, Cookie, so wet my whole hand is soaked because of it."

She gasped out.

"This slick little pussy is the tightest I've ever felt." He slipped another digit into her body and then another until he was thrusting three fingers deep inside of her. He twisted his fingers inside of her and bumped against her G-spot.

"Soon my cock is going to replace these." He emphasized his point by scissoring his fingers inside of her. He moved them faster, harder, and the sound of her flesh sucking at him seemed to fill the room. "Just the feel of your sweet little pussy sucking at these digits could make me come, baby."

She gripped onto his shoulders and dug her nails into his flesh. She found herself wantonly grinding herself on him, moving her hips up and down, and biting her lip to try to hold off from coming a third time. She had never gotten off this many times before, but Kink was merciless as he drew the orgasms out of her easily. He brought his thumb to her clit and started rubbing it back and forth with expert precision. All other thoughts or actions ceased, because in the next second she couldn't stop herself from climaxing. Crying out unabashedly, Cookie pumped her pussy faster and harder on his fingers. He grunted in pleasure against her ear, but never stopped rubbing her. She felt drained in only the best of ways, and had to push his hand away when she became too sensitive. She could hear the almost frantic *thump-thump* of his heart, and she took comfort in knowing that it was just as fast as hers.

There were no coherent thoughts running through her, just mindless need that had her every cell on fire, even after everything Kink had just given her. She opened her eyes and glanced down to see his erection against her thigh. He was so hard for her. She flattened her hands against his chest and gently pushed. When he was on his back she lifted up and stared down the length of his body. Tearing her gaze from the hard length of his cock, she stared into his eyes. Of course, he held an unreadable expression, one that had nothing to do with the shadows playing in the room. The man before her was hard in more ways than one, and he was leaving tonight to do something very dangerous. The thought that this might very well be the last time she saw him weighed heavily on her.

"Baby, stop thinking about what is not right here and right now, okay?" he said softly, and lifted a hand to brush a lock of her hair away.

She nodded, knowing that negative thinking never helped a situation, and in fact only made it worse. She glanced at his shaft and reached out to take hold of the root of it. Kink hissed when she tried to wrap her fingers around the girth, and squeezed. A part of her wanted to please him as much, if not more, than he had pleased her.

She didn't wait for him to say anything, but did notice, even in the darkened room, that he was holding onto the sheets with a white-knuckled grip. Cookie leaned down and brought her mouth to the tip of him. She could feel his heat and opened her mouth wider to flick her tongue over the ridge of the tip. No noise came from him, but he was breathing heavily enough that his abs were clenching with so much force his six-pack was standing out in stark contrast. She wanted him to ache for her like she did for him. Cookie ran her tongue over the flared edge and engulfed him, at least as much as she could. The taste of him exploded in her mouth. It was salty, sweet, and had her pussy becoming wetter for him. She groaned around him and tightened her fingers around the base of his dick. Despite her earlier orgasms, her pussy was drenched and her clit throbbed. She sucked him hard and deep, and when he gripped the back of her head and started thrusting into her mouth, she knew she had power over Kink that most didn't. It was empowering, and she reveled in it. His whole body was strung taut, and she knew he was going to come very soon. He tightened his fingers in her hair, but before she could taste him fully he pushed her back. His breathing was haggard, and the look he gave her heated her entire body.

"On your back with your legs spread, baby." When she did what he said she watched his expression waver for a moment. His gaze dipped between her spread thighs, and he let out a gruff sound. "Jesus, baby." He ran a hand over his mouth. "I want to be inside of you so fucking bad." He slid his gaze to her, and a mask of composure covered his expression instantly. "Tell me you want my cock in you. Tell me how much you want me to be with you."

She had come to learn in this short time that he liked hearing her say these things, and she realized she loved saying them to him.

"Fucking tell me, Cookie, tell me to own it because you freely give yourself to me. Because you're mine."

Oh, God. His words were like gasoline on a fire. It was like he knew exactly what to say to have her on the precipice of climax. "Be inside of me, Kink. Make me yours, and own me because I am freely giving myself to you."

In the next instant his hard body was blanketing hers. He took her mouth in a searing kiss, and she wrapped her hands around his neck, pulling him closer. Cookie's pussy convulsed on its own as the weight of him pushed her into the mattress. He was so much bigger than she was, and his strength was immense. It was hard not to take that into account every time she was with him. But for her there was only Kink, this MC member that didn't take shit from anyone, who was coarse and crude, hard and unforgiving with others, but with her showed a gentler side. He made her feel like she didn't need to have fear when she was with him, and that she was a stronger person than she gave herself credit for her. How strange that she could feel this powerfully for a man that was still so new in her life. . *She* had been the one that decided to take this to the next level, and she wasn't going to sit around and worry about all of the bad things that could happen.

"Make me yours, Kink," she said between kisses, and he groaned out.

He clasped her wrists in one of his hands and brought them above her head. He had told her all the kinky things he liked to do, which was why he was given the nickname by the club. And although one day she wanted to be able to experience everything he had to give in that respect, right now this was enough. She gripped the cold, hard bars of his headboard. A ghost of a smile flittered across his face, as if her act of submission pleased him. When he moved his hands over her collarbones and down to her breasts she closed her eyes and arched her back. Yes, that was what she needed, what she wanted and craved. She yearned to feel his callused hands scrape over her flesh, for him to truly show her what it meant to be cared for in the most primal of ways. He tweaked her nipples, massaged the mounds, and brought a flush of heat to her chest. But the actions he delivered to her were soft, gentle, and didn't have this frantic need pulsing inside of her. It was a slow and steady thump in her body, filing her, claiming her, and bringing her to heights she had never even thought were possible. A wave of lust slammed into her so hard it took her breath away. This wasn't just about having sex, but about giving Kink a part of herself that she had never given to anyone before.

The feel of his erection pressing against her cleft had the desire to rub against him rising to the surface. But she didn't act on her instincts to do that, because she knew that if she was patient and obedient, he would bring her to a place she had never dreamed of.

His warm breath moved across her ear, and she forced herself not to turn toward him. He thrust his hips back and forth against her, slow, easy, but determined and calculated. That wave of power filled her again, and she knew that just because he was the one in control right now, she still held this dominating, hardened biker in the palm of her hand.

"Are you ready for me, Cookie, for this?" He squeezed her breast lightly. "Does the idea of what I do, of what I want to do, scare you?" This man was used to the good, dirty kind of sex. He liked the kind that was kinky and dark, and had always filtered through the back of her mind, but was made up of things she was too afraid to even contemplate. But even though he had asked her a question he didn't give her time to respond. "I'm not any good for you, Cookie, but I'm too selfish to walk away, to let you go." He continued thrusting back and forth against her, making her wetter, hotter. "The world you've lived in has been ugly and cruel, and you deserve something beautiful and light, something that matches who you are." His words were meant to be soft, but she still heard the huskiness in them. "The world *I* live in should scare the hell out of you, not turn you on." His mouth was still by her ear and his hands were still on her breasts. "But you're still here, and you aren't going anywhere, are you, baby?"

She shook her head, not able to speak. His words may have held a note of desperation and despair in them, but his body was still primed for her, just as hers was for him.

"I crave you so fucking bad, and have never wanted someone as much as I want you." He emphasized his point by pressing his erection against her, and a soft sound left her. "I admitted I'm a selfish bastard because, even though I know this is wrong on so many levels, I can't stop. I won't."

"I don't want you to stop." She turned her head and kissed him hard. The sound he made had her heart pounding harder and faster. She didn't want him to stop … ever. "Please, Kink, just take me. I don't care about all of that other stuff."

He slipped his tongue into her mouth at the same time he reached between their bodies and aligned the head of his cock to her entrance. She lifted her hips, knowing that she couldn't take it anymore, and was desperate to feel him stretching her.

"Please—" Her words were cut off when he started to push himself into her nice and easy. She broke the kiss and threw her head back, groaning out her pleasure. When he was fully inside of her he let he let her have a moment of time to get used to him. He then started moving back and forth, making love to her so sweetly that she was gasping for words to tell him what he meant to her. Over and over he pushed into her, and just as slowly he'd pull out. It was a never-ending crescendo of pleasure, one that was meant to titillate and entice her, but not strong enough to get her off. It showed her that he cared for her in his own gruff way, and that he was as capable of giving gently as he was at taking what he wanted.

The minutes ticked by as he made love to her, and for the first time in her life she knew what it really meant.

"I'd die for you," he said against her throat. "I'd kill for you, Bailey." With her hands still securely wrapped around the headboard slats, Kink leaned back only slightly, and looked down to where their bodies were connected. "You're mine and I won't let you go, because I can't. I'm too much of a selfish bastard." And he then started pumping in and out of her. He brought her so close to the edge, and then he'd stop right before he'd continue. Her pussy was so wet for him, and the sound of his skin slapping against hers reverberated in the room.

"All mine." He growled against her neck and picked up speed.

Soon she was falling over the edge into mindless, blissful completion. She let go of the headboard, and grabbed his shoulders, needing to hold onto *him* as she went over. Just as the high started to slowly dwindle, she found herself flipped on her belly. The world shifted beneath her, a gasp left her, and she blinked back the haze that settled over her. He had his hands on her hips, curled his fingers into her flesh, and murmured something she couldn't understand, but she didn't care. All she wanted was to feel him inside of her again. He lifted her ass, palmed her cheeks, and then dipped his finger into her wetness, only to bring it to her back entrance. Cookie knew what he wanted, and she shouldn't have wanted *that*. But she did. She shouldn't have wanted any more, especially what she knew was about to come, but she couldn't stop herself from giving him everything.

"You going to give me this, baby?" He squeezed one cheek of her ass, and used the finger of his other hand to tease her anus.

She didn't answer verbally, but showed him with her body language that she wanted this, too. Palms flat on the mattress and legs spread wide, she waited for him to make his next move. Cookie looked over her shoulder, saw that he was staring at her ass, and waited with her heart in her throat for him to take her. She wasn't an anal virgin, but this was the first time she'd craved it. Her vagina still convulsed from the after tremors of her orgasm, and she still had her ass high in the air for the taking. The thought of letting him in there, with his massive erection, should have scared the hell out of her, but all she felt was the mindless pleasure of wanting more.

Cookie closed her eyes when she felt his fingers skate over her slit to gather her cream. There was no tensing, no worries about what was going to happen next as he spread her juices over her anus. The sheets were tightly fisted between her fingers, and he repeated the action, over and over, bringing her closer to begging him to fuck her ass. She thought he would push right into her, but instead he leaned over her, covered her back with his chest, and breathed into her ear. With his other hand she felt him stroke her lower back, and she knew it wasn't because he liked that part of her body. She had scars there, and he had obviously seen them. This small act of sweetness had tears forming in her eyes, but she blinked them away.

"You still with me?" he asked softly.

"I am. Please don't stop."

"Okay, baby." He teased her back hole again, slow, easy, gently. "Just stay here with me, okay?"

She nodded.

Of course the fear of pain was present, but his soft touches told her he was a dominating, but gentle and compassionate lover. He had already ensured her pleasure above his by bringing her to climax three times, and he still had yet to find his own release.

"You're so responsive to my touch. Will you be this responsive when I'm buried deep in your ass?"

A shiver shook her body. She didn't answer, couldn't.

"Come on, Cookie," he said softly. "Answer me." His voice was thick and sweet like honey.

"I want to feel you everywhere." She felt herself blush, not because she had said the words he so desperately wanted to hear, but because she had meant them, each and every one.

"I am so hard for you. Do you feel what you do to me?" He lifted off her back, and she felt his erection slide across her ass.

She wanted to tell him to do it, to beg him to end her misery and quit taunting her. Maybe she spoke aloud because in the next second he was moving away from her only long enough to grab some lube and a condom from his bedside table. He was back to her seconds later, and poured the cold, slick lubrication between her cheeks. The feel of his cockhead pressed to her anus when he was finished priming her had her breathing heavier. He slowly pushed all his hard inches into her. Tears stung her eyes, and she started to feel the burn of being filled completely.

The sting of the tip of his shaft popping through the tight ring of muscle had her squeezing her eyes shut. And then he slid easily into her. A groan left him, and he held onto her hips in an ironclad grip. He didn't move for a few seconds, and she knew he was letting her body get accustomed to his girth.

"So good, Bailey, so fucking good that I could come right now." He started moving in and out of her, and soon the burn of pain was replaced by something far more pleasing. Each time he pushed into her that desire heightened. His groans behind her were enough to have her nearing yet another orgasm, but it was his hands reaching in front of her and rubbing her clit back and forth that had her crying out. She pressed her face into the mattress and shook uncontrollably. One thrust, two thrusts, and on the third one he buried himself so deep in her ass that his balls slapped her pussy. His language was crass, but it reflected the strong emotions she was sure he felt at that moment. She couldn't fault him for that, because inside she felt the same way. When he pulled out of her and wrapped his body around hers, she had to force herself to not fall into a euphoric-induced coma.

"You leave soon," she said softly, and closed her eyes when he kissed the top of her head, and shifted enough to bring the blanket over them both.

"I know."

"Are you frightened about what will happen tonight?" She leaned back enough that she could tilt her head back and look at him. "I'm frightened for you." She knew telling him that wasn't helping anything, but the words had tumbled out of her mouth.

He didn't speak for several seconds and then cupped the side of her face. He looked right into her eyes, like he could see her very soul. "Am I scared of dying, or taking a life that crossed the club?" He shook his head.

"No, baby, I'm not scared. I'm juiced to get this over with, to get vengeance for what they did to us." He smoothed his thumb along her cheekbone. "I want to make sure you're safe, that Callie is safe." He smiled, but it faltered slightly. "But I will tell you what I am afraid of." He leaned in close enough that their lips touched. "I'm scared of leaving you behind." He kissed her hard, possessively, and with so much emotion that she tasted the saltiness of her tears. For once in her life she had let her guard down, her carefully placed wall that she had survived with. And it was all because of this one man and the powerful emotions he evoked inside of her.

Chapter Twelve

Everything was quiet, too fucking quiet for Kink's comfort. He stood beside Lucien, and Malice was on the other side of him. Tuck, Rock, and Ruin were spread out around them, and the sound of several men inhaling from their cigarettes was loud in the still night. Gravel crunching under tires had all of them turning around. A dark van came to a stop beside their own black one parked just a few feet away. They had left their bikes behind at the clubhouse, because what they were going for was stealth, not power. They didn't want their spot compromised if the cult was in the warehouse, which they didn't even know for sure since they didn't have a visual of cars or activity in the rundown building.

Jagger and his crew stepped out of the van and made their way toward them. The Grizzly MC was one fierce bunch of motherfuckers, having this animal power to back them up, and so they were an asset and hardcore alley to have behind The Brothers of Menace. Jagger stopped, and Stinger, Diesel, Dallas, Court, Drevin, and Brick all stopped beside their President. The shadows played over their massive bodies, and although most residents of Steel Corner and even River Run were afraid of this MC, The Brothers could take care of their own and handle their shit.

"Thanks for the back-up, boys," Lucien said and flicked his cigarette away. The moon was full, and even though it cast this silvery glow on everything, with the buildings scattered around this industrial part of town, everything looked more sinister. Good, because they all were a sinister fucking bunch. The Fairview chapter had come in earlier in the day, and they stood back as they moved closer to The Grizzlies.

"You know we have your back. Your club helped us out during some tricky shit, and things will be a lot better if we work together instead of against each other."

Kink couldn't agree more. He shoved his hands in his front pockets and glanced at the six Grizzlies in front of them.

"So, how is this going down?" Jagger asked. "Lucien, you told us the bare minimum on the phone." Jagger rolled his head around on his neck and then cracked his knuckles. There was this dangerous, hard, and angry energy that was coming off of everyone, but what they were about to do was not light work. People would get killed, but when someone fucked with the club, with the people they had under their protection, action had to be taken.

"We don't have confirmation that they are in there right now. We haven't seen any movement on the outside, and there are no vehicles parked there," Kink said, and glanced at the men standing around. Marx and the rest of the Fairview chapter moved closer. They had already gone through all of this with them, but they needed to formulate the plan now.

"I want the Fairview boys to head around the back, spread out so the side and any exits are covered, and then Jagger and The Grizzlies will head with us to get inside," Lucien said, his voice low, and reflecting all of his anger. "I know my boys, and me, want to take these fuckers out hard and fast, but we need to play it safe." Lucien glanced around, too.

"They've been quiet, probably hiding out for the most part after the bombing," Kink said, wanting nothing more than to just go in there and start shooting. Cookie could have been in the cabin when those heartless sons-of-bitches blew up their shit, and that thought had him curling his hands in rage. He had left his woman at the clubhouse, tucked in his bed, with her red hair fanned out over his pillows, and her breathing easy. He had fucked her every which way, and claimed her so hard there was no doubt she was his. And then she had asked if he was afraid of going out tonight. Although this was club business, the women in the club, and the guys' family members, knew why they had been there, and knew what the members were going to do.

Retaliate.

"And then what?" Stinger asked and exhaled a puff of smoke. "What the fuck then?"

"What do you mean?" Kink asked, not about to play these stupid little games with the biker.

Stinger took a step forward and shrugged. "I just mean, what the fuck you boys plan on doing if they are inside?" Stinger said, and kept his expression stoic.

"We take them out, easy as that," Kink said just as stoically. He had a Glock tucked at the small of his back and a knife strapped to his waist. The other Brothers had guns as well, and they were just as anxious to get this fucking going as he was. Marx and his guys moved closer, and although the cult had started on their territory first weeks ago, those bastards had come to River Run, and weren't going to leave.

"We've been watching the perimeter for the last twenty minutes, and there hasn't been any movement, but we assume they are operating at full force inside." Lucien took out his gun, lifted the SIG Sauer, and checked the bullets.

"And you're sure they are the ones that bombed your place?" Jagger asked.

Lucien put his gun in the waistband of his pants and glared at Jagger. "You questioning me now, Grizzly?" Lucien took a step closer, and Kink moved forward. Over the last week Lucien had been acting strange as hell. But

Kink just assumed it was all the crap happening lately and the stress and pressure weighing on the club. "We have the proof that they bought the bomb materials only days before they fucked up our shit, even saw the blueprints that had of the cabin they used the explosives on."

Jagger lifted his hands in surrender, but smirked. "Hey, we are here to help you, not fight with you. I was just asking, but if you say they fucked you over, then they fucked you over, man." Jagger's grin widened, and the rest of The Grizzlies chuckled. "Listen, let's just get this done, because I want to get home and see my old lady, okay?"

Lucien exhaled and nodded. "Yeah, I think we are all wound tight right now."

The two Presidents spoke for a few more minutes on the details, and Kink glanced at the warehouse once more. "Listen, you all know that this is going to be heavy when we get in there, find them, and they realize we are there for payback."

"How about we quit talking about this, and tear them apart?" Stinger asked, inhaled from his joint once more, and flicked it aside.

No one argued.

They all checked their weapons, and Marx and his men went in first. Even from the distance Kink could see them working in perfect formation as they moved around the sides of the building, and then disappeared from their sight. Lucien turned and looked at Kink. "Once we get the call from Marx that they are set then we'll move in."

Kink nodded. They stood still, tense, and ready for action. Minutes passed, and then the buzzing sound coming from inside Lucien's cut had even the air stilling. Kink looked at Lucien, watched him accept the call and place the phone to his ear, and then there was silence.

"Hold on. I want you to relay this to the guys." Lucien put the phone on speaker, and Marx started talking.

"We're in position, and from my standpoint I can see through a side window there appears to be one of them standing guard. It looks like he's packing a shotgun, maybe more, but it's too dark, and he's too far for me to see exactly," Marx said softly.

"Can you see if there are any more in the warehouse?" Malice said in a gruff voice.

There was a moment of silence, and then Marx was speaking again. "I can see shadows in the room the bastard is clearly guarding, but I couldn't give you an exact head count."

"Okay, keep your position," Lucien said, ended the call, and put the cell back in his pocket. "Now, I want to be sure we are dealing with the cult fuckers when we bust in there. Play it safe, be careful, and only shoot the ones going after us."

"And if there are females and children in there?" Jagger asked. "Because we don't hurt women and children."

"And you think we do?" Lucien said on a growl.

"No, but I want to make it clear that we won't be a part of that, and won't allow it to happen."

Lucien shook his head. "No worries about that. Marx has a few guys that will get any women or children out, if they are in there. They will be taken away from the violence."

Jagger nodded and grunted. "Okay, good, then let's get this fucking moving."

They all headed toward the front of the building silently, stealthily. Kink, as well as the other men, all kept their gazes moving back and forth. They were close to the front bay doors, and pressed their bodies to the rusted and dented metal. Lucien gestured for Kink to move forward.

Kink grabbed his Glock and moved past the other men. He scanned the perimeter, saw shadows pass across the roof, and pressed his back to the wall once more. The other bikers had their guns raised, their expressions alert, and ready for violence. Kink reached out and tried the door that was beside him. It was stuck, but after he put some weight and strength into it the heavy metal pushed open. He scanned the rooftop again, but everything was silent. Either this cult was too convinced they were safe here, and therefore didn't need security, or they knew The Brothers and The Grizzlies were here, and waited for them inside.

The other bikers moved behind Kink, and he took one deep breath before slipping into the dark building.

****

Cookie was nervous as hell and had to have checked the clock a hundred times already. The guys had only been gone an hour, but it felt like it had been eternity. She had fallen asleep in Kink's arms after he thoroughly pleased her. But she had woken up alone, cold, and feeling this sick dread in her belly. So she had gotten dressed and went into the main room, expecting to be alone, but finding Callie, Tatum, Adrianna, and Molly out there drinking alcohol and looking grim as hell.

They looked how Cookie felt.

Cookie contemplated going over to the bar instead of sitting on the couch with them. She might know the women fairly well, aside from Kink's daughter, but she didn't want to intrude on them. But when she turned and headed toward the bar for a drink herself, Tatum called out.

"Cookie, come over here and take a few sips off of this."

She turned and stared at Tatum who held up a bottle of Tullamore Irish whiskey.

Cookie wasn't much of a drinker, but her nerves were so shot that she needed something to help settle them. She walked over to the women and sat down beside Molly. Tatum handed over the bottle, and without thinking Cookie brought it to her lips and took a long drink. The liquor was smooth and instantly warmed her, but she had never liked the taste of alcohol, and started coughing a bit because of it. Callie reached out and took the bottle with a smile, and then took several long pulls from it.

"Easy, girl. Your dad would kill me if he knew I was allowing you to drink."

Callie handed the bottle to Tatum. "No, I think he'd be okay since I am at the clubhouse doing it. Besides," Callie shrugged and looked down at her bare feet. "I'm really nervous about what they are doing, and if they will even come back." She looked at each of them. "I mean, this is their life, our life. I know that, and although I don't know exactly what they went to do, we all know they went after that cult." Callie swallowed audibly. "I'm worried about my dad, about the club, and about Lucien." Callie glanced up with just her eyes, and Cookie saw this strange expression cross the young woman's face after she said Lucien's name. Callie cleared her throat, leaned back on the couch, and tucked her feet under her bottom.

Cookie knew that look well. It was one that she had covering her own face far too many times whenever she thought about Kink.

"I'm just worried about everyone." Callie started twisting her hands in her lap. It was clear there was something going on with Callie and Lucien by the way the girl acted when she just said his name. Sure, they were all worried, but the way Callie reacted was the behavior of a woman who worried for a man she wanted.

For the man she loved. How far things went with her and Lucien Cookie didn't know, and maybe Callie just had a crush on The Brothers of Menace President, but either way there was something there.

"Momma."

The little voice came from upstairs, and Cookie looked up to see Dakota standing there.

"Baby, you need to go to sleep." Molly stood and went to Dakota. She picked up the little boy and cradled him.

"Momma, I want Daddy."

"Dakota, Daddy had to leave, and he won't be back until morning." She pushed away the dark hair from his forehead. "If you go back to sleep morning will come quicker."

Dakota shook his head. "I want Stinger, then, Momma. I want a story. I can't sleep." Dakota whined.

"Stinger isn't here either, sweetheart. Come on, honey, let's go back to bed. I'll sing you a song."

"Twinkle, Twinkle, Momma."

Cookie watched Molly slip down the upstairs hallway and take Dakota to bed. What would it be like to have a little person that relied solely on her for everything? She had never worried about any of that. It was a frightening thought to have to care for someone other than herself, but Cookie thought about the joys it would bring as well.

"I'll be back. Need to use the restroom." Tatum rose and left her, Callie, and Adrianna alone. Adrianna was quiet, probably so damn worried for Malice. Cookie reached out and grabbed the other woman's hand, and Adrianna glanced up and gave her a tight smile. Cookie turned and stared at Callie, it was to see the girl staring at her.

"So, you and my dad, huh?" Callie said matter-of-factly and shifted on the couch to see Cookie better.

"Excuse me?" Of course she wouldn't deny it, because it wasn't like she was trying to hide anything, but she also wasn't going to talk about this with a seventeen-year-old.

"I mean, you don't have to say it or anything, because it's not my business, but I can see the way you two look at each other. And then of course there is the talk around the clubhouse."

Cookie stared at Callie and reached for the bottle of Irish whiskey. "Well, you got one thing right, it really isn't your business." She glanced at Callie and saw her smiling, and so she did the same. "But, yeah, I guess Kink and I are…" She shrugged, now knowing if she should put a label to it.

"You're his old lady," Callie said flatly. "I get it. Everyone here does. If you're in the biker life, and your man wants you, that's what you are to him."

Cookie nodded. "Yeah, Kink called me that, and I want to be that with him … for him." She took a long drink of the whiskey and then handed it to Callie. "What about you?"

"What about me?" Callie said softly, and then took a long swig of the liquor, too.

"You into this whole lifestyle? You have an old man, if that's what they're called?"

Callie looked down and shook her head. "No, I just graduated, will be eighteen soon, and just want to live my life." She looked at Cookie. "Besides, these men, the ones that are in the MC…" She licked her lips. "Once you're theirs, you're *theirs*, if you know what I mean."

Cookie slowly nodded. "What about Lucien?" Cookie asked hesitantly, not knowing if she had read Callie wrong, or if she was crossing a line.

Callie looked uncomfortable all of a sudden, and Cookie knew it was because she'd mentioned Lucien. But before Callie could even respond, Cookie heard her cell going off. The other girl grabbed her phone off the table between them, saw the number, and knitted her brows.

"Hello?" Callie said after she accepted the call. Callie was silent for several minutes, and then she pulled the phone away from her ear, stared at it, and then let it drop to the floor.

"Callie, God, what's wrong?" Cookie said and moved closer, fearing that she had just gotten a call that Kink and the other men were… She shook her head, not about to think about that, or even contemplate that Kink was dead. "Callie, honey, talk to me." She grabbed her shoulders, shook her slightly, and tried to get through the clear shock that had taken over Callie.

Molly finally came back downstairs, and Tatum finished up in the bathroom. Adrianna followed shortly after.

Kendra, probably the youngest girl that had been in Denver when the pimp had attacked them, came out of one of the rooms. She stopped, looked at everyone, and said, "Oh, God, more bad news?"

And then when Harlem, another young girl from the house, shuffled behind Kendra, Cookie could have screamed. This wasn't a fucking circus, yet there were now several women staring at them. They all wore either confused or worried expressions, and Cookie hadn't even heard what the news was Callie had just gotten. Cookie glanced away from the women, and looked back at the young girl. "Callie, sweetheart, please tell me what's going on."

Callie looked at Cookie, opened her mouth, and promptly shut it. She closed her eyes, and these two big tears slipped out of the corner of them. Cookie felt that dread fill her to the point she felt like she was suffocating from it all. Her throat tightened, and just staring at Callie, and seeing the pain cover her face, Cookie just wanted to take the girl in her arms and comfort her.

When Callie opened her mouth again, this gasping sound left her. She scrubbed her hand over her face, and Cookie saw the way her hands shook. She stared right at Cookie, and the color of her eyes looked so much like Kink's. "That was the police." Callie swallowed audibly again. "My mom and Dale are dead."

Chapter Thirteen

Kink was in front, with Lucien, the rest of The Brothers, and Jagger and his men following closely behind. They were not some kind of trained SWAT team, but they were organized, and had the same goal in mind: end this now so no one else got hurt. This cult had stirred up shit in Fairview, and although Kink hadn't been there, he had heard from Malice and the other guys what the cult had done. This "church" had a one-track mindset, one that was toxic, vile, and screamed it was their way or no way. The Brothers would have just turned their back on their hateful protesting, but the cult had taken it way over the fucking line, and now it was time to get their answers, and make them see that once they screwed with the MC, they were dead.

Kink stopped, which caused the rest of the guys to do the same. He was just about to round a corner when he saw the slight shadow move across the wall, and heard the shuffling of someone moving closer. Marx's men were standing on the other side of the building, waiting for the action to start so they could move in and take out anyone vulnerable. He turned and glanced at Lucien who was directly behind him. The President of the club looked hard, tense. They gave each other a brisk nod, not that they could read each other's minds, but because they knew what they needed to do.

Kink stepped around the corner, gun trained straight in front of him, and the only light coming from one of the broken skylights above him. The man who stood only a few feet from them had his back to Kink, but upon hearing something behind him the man turned. For a moment all they did was stare at each other. The MC men wouldn't react until Kink or this fucker made the first move. But the man didn't move so much as a muscle for a long minute, and then his smile spread, as if he had been expecting Kink.

"Welcome, brother." The cult member smiled wider, and from the corner of his eye Kink saw the guy's fingers move. "Before this is over with you will be the ones kneeling before us, and accepting our way." The man lifted his gun, but Kink was the one to react faster.

He shot his gun right when the cult member lifted his and aimed it right at Kink's chest. The sound of the bullet leaving his Glock ricocheted off the metal wall, and had this ringing settling in his ears. It was like a giant tuning fork had been hit, and they were stuck in the center of it. The MCs reacted, moved behind Kink, and then they went forward in unison. The cult member lay on the floor groaning. Kink hadn't killed him, but he had incapacitated him with a bullet to his knee.

"Where is the fucker that is leading you and these lemmings?" Lucien said in a deep, deadly voice.

Kink was on alert, watching the narrow hallway and listening for any movement up ahead. He turned around, saw Jagger and his boys scanning the area behind them, and knew they were watching as well.

"You are all nothing but cattle in all of this," the man said again, and then moaned out and clutched his knee. "We knew you'd come to us after you received our message."

There was a low hiss that came from Lucien, but Kink focused before him. Malice was beside him, and Rock came up on the other side of Kink. He glanced over his shoulder quickly.

"Where is he?" Lucien leaned down on his haunches and moved close enough that he was right in the man's face. "You think you're in pain now, you haven't felt anything yet." Lucien wrapped his hand around the guy's throat.

"Lucien, we need to keep moving. They no doubt heard the gun, and the longer we sit here with this piece of shit, the more time they have to prepare for us."

Lucien didn't move for a suspended second, and when it was clear they weren't going to get any answers out of the cult member aside from Lucien clocked him right in the fucking face.

"We welcome the pain because that is the will of the mighty, but heed our words, and know that when this is all said and done your bodies, and the ones of those whores you protect and make money off of, will be lying at our feet."

And then Malice was moving toward Lucien and the man, lifting his gun, and putting a bullet in the guy's head. The cult member fell to the ground on his side.

"Damn, man," Lucien said and slowly rose to stand. "Nice fucking shot." Lucien clapped Malice on the shoulder. Everyone stared at the body on the ground, but then snapped into motion. They didn't waste another second in moving down the hallway, but when they rounded a corner they faced off with a man standing before an entryway. The light from the room behind him shone brightly, and the chanting that came forward was loud but muffled. But the man didn't raise the gun he had strapped to his side. Instead he moved to the side and gestured them forward. Brick was on the guy a second later, taking him down as if he were nothing more than an annoying fly.

"Brothers, there is no need for violence." The deep, male voice came through the open entryway, and the sound of the men grabbing their guns and aiming them was loud behind Kink. "But we will engage if that is the will of our Master. Enter, show yourselves, and let us worship the good and only."

They could see the man speaking, the one who was clearly the leader as he wore this bright white robe, had this large wooden cross hanging from his neck, and had about twenty men standing behind him in dark hooded cloaks. None of the MC men said anything, but Kink felt their anger, felt the violence brewing right below the surface. It was the same thing he felt, the same hatred he had for these men he didn't even know.

"That's him, that's the motherfucker that was leading these washouts in Fairview," Malice said as he moved up closer beside Kink. He glanced at Malice, saw his jaw locked up tight, and then lowered his gaze to his hand only to see his knuckles bone white from holding the gun tightly.

"You followed us from Fairview, came to our territory, and spouted your holier-than-thou bullshit," Malice gritted out, and Lucien reached out and grabbed his forearm.

"Easy, brother."

Kink took a step to the side and let Lucien move forward. "You knew we were here," Lucien stated matter-of-factly.

The leader nodded, and his grin widened. "We knew that the bombing would get your attention, and we have come to learn that you and your little congregation are in desperate need of our guidance." The leader stepped back, and the dark robbed men moved an inch forward.

Kink and the other MC members lifted their guns, but the leader *tsked* and shook his head.

"Brothers, we are here to save you, to bring you redemption for your sins, and help you see the light."

"Motherfucker, the only thing we are going to be doing is taking you down," Lucien gritted out, and Kink knew that the showdown was going to happen any minute now. Everyone was barely leashing in their rage as they stared at the bastards that thought destroying their property and putting innocent lives in danger was "saving them".

"Join us and put away all of your filthy and immoral ways of earning a living." The leader grinned. "Be one of us or fall like the banished angel from heaven."

"Oh man, this is like a really bad and twisted afterschool special," Stinger said from behind Kink.

"You have to be high, drunk, and deranged to think we came here to join your little fucking cult," Malice said. The men removed their hoods, and Kink was relieved to see there were no women or children amongst them.

"That little explosion was a threat, a warning that we will not stand by and let this world get sent down to the pits of hell by the likes of you and your kind."

"Our kind?" Jagger was the one to speak, and The Grizzly leader looked two seconds away from tearing through his skin.

"The kind that sells women for pleasure, deals with drugs, guns, and the like. You and yours are a stain upon humanity, and the sooner you are eradicated, the sooner this world can get back on the right track, too."

"You piece of shit," Rock growled out, and before Kink knew what was happening Rock had fired a shot. The next sequence of events happened fast. The large room was filled with shouting and gunfire. Kink and Lucien moved to the side, and he pressed his back to the metal beam.

"Go around, Kink, take out as many of these bastards as you can." A bullet slammed into the concrete in front of them, and Kink and Lucien both ducked.

"Where the fuck were they hiding those guns?" Kink asked and leaned to the side, and saw the cult members no longer wore their dark robes. They held shotguns and 9mm handguns, and Kink realized these fuckers had them hidden under their cloaks the whole time.

"Man, these guys are fucking psycho," Lucien said and ducked just as a stray bullet slammed into the wall beside him. "And they're dead."

Kink nodded at Lucien, and they both turned and faced off with the firing squad. Jagger and his men were taking care of several of them, and The Brothers had the other half, but there were three men, including that fucking crazy ass leader, who were coming toward him and Lucien. Kink fired off a shot and took out the guy to the right. Lucien put a bullet in the head of the guy on the left. The bodies stacked up on the ground, and several of Marx's men came running in through a side door. Blood thickened the air in a tangy, metallic scent that was nauseating, but familiar. Soon the large warehouse room was filled with Brothers of Menace and Grizzly bikers. Everyone was breathing hard, and they slowly moved forward, circling the leader, who wore this cocky smile on his face.

"Brothers, children of the light, we are one." The leader held his arms up above his head, tipped his chin up, and closed his eyes.

"Motherfucker, you're about to be another body on this ground." Lucien moved forward, cocked his gun, and stopped when he was a foot from the leader.

"Tobias, my brother. My name is Tobias." The leader grinned. "You can kill me, lay my body with my brethren, but I won't be the one that judges you. That bomb should have killed you and all of your fucking whores," Tobias snarled out. "And if I had to do over again, I would have taken the bitches out myself, and rid the world of their disgusting and nasty lives on this earth."

"Well, well, well, looks like the asshole's true colors are coming out," Ruin said on a humorless laugh.

"I don't need any other reason to have done what I did other than the fact I am doing my God's work."

"Motherfucker, I should make you suffer for all your bullshit," Lucien said, and in the next instance backhanded Tobias so hard the leader fell backward. The deadly silence filled the room. Kink clutched the gun and felt his skin pull taut with the need riding high in him to just shoot the asshole.

"Why would you follow us? You could have done your creepy, demented shit back in Utah, but you traveled here to, what? End up with my gun pointed to your head and two seconds away from tasting the bullet?" Lucien snarled out, and lifted the gun. "If you would have stayed in Fairview and minded your own fucking business you wouldn't be about to die right now. But you put the people that are my family in danger, and because of that I will not show you any mercy."

"You can kill me, but there will be more like me, more that will come and get rid of the —"

Lucien pressed the gun to Tobias's head, and in one, swift move pulled the trigger.

Tobias fell backward, and blood immediately started to pool beneath his skull. The silence stretched throughout the room. Marx and then a few of his last remaining men who had been outside came in. Kink looked away from the corpses on the ground and stared at Marx and his men that were surveying the room.

"Well, fuck, you guys took them out fast." Marx strapped his gun to his thigh. "And made one big fuckin' mess." He started chuckling, and although some of his men followed suit, Kink didn't find this situation amusing in the least.

Yeah, these men deserved to die for what they did, for what they could have done, but taking a life was never easy. It chipped away at a person's soul, and Kink had killed more people than he even cared to think about. Did he even have a soul? Did he even know what was right from wrong anymore? He watched Malice move over to the leader. The other biker kicked the shit out of Tobias's body, and the anger that came from Malice was tangible. But then again Kink would have felt the same mind-numbing rage if he had been standing with Cookie so close to the bombing.

"I got a guy that lives in Steamboat that cleans shit up like this," Marx said and grabbed his cell from inside of his cut. "You think this is the end of it?" he asked no one in particular.

Kink looked at Tobias, who stared up at him with his now cold, lifeless eyes. The man had shown no fear, and in fact almost seemed like he was embracing death. If he had been anyone else Kink might have respected the hell out of that attitude, but as it was, and because of what this bastard had done, Kink couldn't care less. He turned his head and spit out a mouthful of spit and blood, felt his jaw ache from the right hook that asshole had given him, and moved away from the bodies. Now that this was over with, well, for now at least, Kink just wanted to get back to the clubhouse and be with his woman and his daughter. He looked at Marx who had moved closer.

"You think there are more of these hacks walking around?" Marx stared at him and grinned.

"There is always more, man." Kink looked back at Tobias one more time. "And it's never over with, not for us anyway." There was a noise from a backroom, but when everyone turned to look that way the sound of a gun going off echoed through the room. Kink had his gun out and trained on the dark entryway in a matter of seconds, he saw another man in a dark robe—the same as the once living cult fuckers. Without thinking and only reacting, Kink fired off a shot. The guy went down with a bullet to his head, like the rest of his cult brethren. The weird silence that filled the room had Kink turning and staring at the men behind him. They were all staring at the same thing … Lucien. Kink looked at the President, saw the other man holding his thigh, and then saw the blood starting to seep down his pants and cover the floor.

"Fuck, the bastard got me," Lucien said on a snarl, and removed his hand from his leg. The blood spread even quicker, and Lucien covered his thigh again. "Fuck." And then he went down.

Chapter Fourteen

Cookie held Callie, and although she was exhausted, it was mainly from having to listen to the young woman cry for the last two hours. She looked down at her sweet, sleeping face, and reached down to push some dark hair away from her face. Even as she slept Callie's pain could be seen and felt.

"How is she doing?" Tatum said and moved up to sit in the chair across from her. It was going on five in the morning, and the sun was just starting to rise over the mountains in the horizon.

Cookie shrugged. "Okay now that she is sleeping, but I can't imagine how she'll handle this in the days, weeks, hell, years to come."

Tatum nodded and grabbed the blanket that was over the back of her chair. She moved over to Callie and placed it over the girl. Tatum might have been well into her forties, but she was gorgeous with this long blonde hair she kept braided a lot of the time, and this curvy body that said she took care of herself.

Cookie was sitting on the leather couch with Callie sprawled out beside her, with her head in her lap. Harlem was sleeping on the other couch across the room, and Kendra was lying beside her. After Callie had broken down after saying her mother had died, Molly and Adrianna had tried to comfort the young girl, but she'd seemed inconsolable. Finally Molly left to go upstairs to take care of a crying Dakota. That was when Cookie had brought the girl close to her, wrapped her arms around Callie, and just held her. No one had done something like this to her when she was Callie's age, and it felt good to ease someone, even for a small moment.

"I know Callie and her mom weren't close, and she wanted to leave Sarah because they didn't get along, but I can't imagine losing my mom at such a young age, and in a horrific car crash either." Tatum had lowered her voice to a whisper, and the empathy on her face was tangible.

Cookie looked down at Callie and nodded at what the other woman had said. Once Callie had been able to speak through her tears enough to tell them what had happened, Cookie had found out that Sarah and her boyfriend Dale had been driving home from a party. Dale had been drunk, lost control of the car, and went through a guardrail. Then they had crashed into a ravine, and died instantly. At least there was that one solace for Callie in knowing her mother hadn't suffered. But they hadn't been able to get a hold of Kink, and although now was not the time to bring this up to Kink, this was something that couldn't have waited.

Cookie looked down at Callie again, and just as she was about to push more of Callie's hair away Molly came rushing down the stairs, Adrianna right behind her, with frantic looks on their faces.

"What's wrong?" Tatum was up and moving toward the other woman. "Shit, we don't need any more bad news."

Callie stirred and slowly woke, and then shot up and started breathing hard. "What's the matter?" She looked back and forth, still slightly sleepy and confused. Cookie rubbed her back, trying to ease her. Callie looked over, her eyes red-rimmed and swollen, and her face slightly puffy from crying. "I had a dream, one where there was so much death and blood."

"It's okay." But that was a lie. Cookie knew this situation was about to get worse before it got better. Molly moved over to the front door, opened it, and wrapped her arms around her waist.

Cookie stood, but kept Callie close to her. "Molly, what happened?" She stepped up beside the other woman and glanced outside. The sun was rising about the mountains now, but there was no comfort in the light and warmth, not right now at least.

Molly turned toward Cookie, glanced at Callie, and then said, "Lucien's been shot."

Cookie felt Callie tense, and then lean into her, as if she couldn't stand.

"Is he d-dead?" Callie asked softly, and if Cookie had any second thoughts about the girl wanting Lucien, she didn't have them now. Because this wasn't about Callie being worried about a man she cared about as family. Cookie could hear that clearly in the other woman's voice. Callie's emotions were as clear as day, and when Cookie looked at Molly she saw the club nurse looking a little confused, as if she could tell there was a little more behind Callie's statement than just those spoken words.

Molly shook her head and swallowed. "No, honey, but I don't know how bad the wound is. They called in Malcolm's dad, and the doctor should be here soon."

"My dad's okay? The other guys, too?" Callie asked softly.

"As far as I know." Molly turned and faced outside again. The sound of the gates being opened by two prospects, and of tires squealing on the concrete as the two vans sped up to the house surrounded them almost ominously. Molly, Adrianna, and Tatum were already out the front door and racing toward the vans, before Cookie led Callie outside. She wanted to rush to the guys, make sure they were okay, that Kink was okay, and hold him tightly. But Callie had a death grip on her, was shaking, and she knew the girl needed a stable post right now. Cookie seemed to be that for her right now, and she wasn't going to abandon her.

"Oh God." Her heart slammed hard against her ribs, and sweat bloomed along her forehead as she watched all these bikers pile out of the vans. She didn't know many of them. But her main focus was on Kink. He was one of the guys who helped lift Lucien out of the back of one of the vehicles, and a gasping sob left Callie.

"We need to go to them," Callie said, but didn't move.

"I know, honey, but right now we'll be in the way. They need to take care of Lucien, and I have no medical training to help in this." She looked at Molly who stopped off to the side looking worried as hell. "Molly, do you need an extra set of hands?" Cookie might not know what the hell she would be doing, but she could hand stuff to her if need be.

Molly shrugged, rubbed the center of her chest, and then moved over to them. "I might, but I need to assess Lucien, see how bad it is, and hopefully get him stable. The doctor should be here any minute, but stay close, okay?"

Cookie nodded, and Adrianna moved closer to them.

"What if he dies?" Callie pulled away and stared at Cookie with these huge blue eyes. The young woman probably felt the world on her shoulders right now. Cookie knew she felt that way right now. This girl loved the President of The Brothers of Menace. That much was clear. It wasn't about knowing him her whole life. It was about a hell of a lot more than that.

"It'll be okay," Adrianna said. "It has to be okay." Cookie wrapped her arm around Callie's shoulder, pulled her in tight, and tried to give her the comfort she needed. Kink scanned the grounds almost frantically, and when he stopped his gaze right on them, there was this relief that could be clearly seen. Callie took off toward him, but she stopped when she was a foot from all of the other guys. There was just too much going on right now. With the yelling, action, and a lifeless Lucien in the guys' arms, everything seemed to happen slowly. But at the same time everything seemed to be speeding up faster than she could even comprehend.

"Callie, I need you to wait over there while we get Lucien taken care of, okay sweetheart?" Kink said in passing, and then he looked at Cookie once more. There was this pain, this hardened expression, and this violence that still covered his face.

Cookie went over to Callie, embraced her again, and stared at the men as they took Lucien into the oversized garage. The sound of an approaching car had her looking behind her and seeing a flashy looking SUV pull to a stop behind the vans. The doctor, she assumed, took off toward the garage with an oversized bag in hand.

"Come on, just in case they need us." They both all but ran toward the garage, and she yelled over her shoulder when she saw the girls that had been inside of the house open the back door. "Stay inside, and start making some breakfast for the guys." She saw Kendra holding Dakota, and was thankful he was in safe arms right now. Cookie let go of Callie and went into the garage. They had Lucien up on a stainless steel table, and had everything off of him. Seeing a man as strong and powerful as Lucien lying there naked and vulnerable, with a bullet hole in his leg, shook Cookie to her core. Blood seeped out of him and started to pool on the table beneath him. Reality crashed into Cookie, and she pushed Callie away from it all. Fortunately, the young girl didn't object.

"I need everyone out except the nurse, and a few of the guys that can help hand supplies to me," the doctor yelled out, and all of the men started coming toward her. Cookie moved out of their way, and when Pierce grabbed her arm gently and steered her out as well, she glanced behind her and saw that Kink and Malice had stayed behind.

"Come on, there isn't anything for us to do in there besides get in their way."

She knew Pierce was right, but she didn't want to leave. She wanted to help, even if she didn't know anything about this shit or saving someone's life. The guys didn't go far though. They stayed over by the back of the clubhouse, smoking and glancing at the garage. The sound of yet another approaching car had Cookie glancing up from where she had buried her head in Callie's hair. A white van came right up to the garage, turned around, and backed up toward the door. The young man she had seen briefly yesterday, Malcolm she thought his name was, got out of the vehicle and moved toward the so fast it seemed to happen within seconds. He started carrying medical equipment, and even a cooler inside of the garage, and then it was back to everyone waiting.

"This is fucked up, man," Pierce said to no one in particular.

"This is more than fucked up," Tuck said and inhaled from a joint he was smoking.

"What if he doesn't make it—"

The look Tuck gave Rock was enough to shut the man up. "We aren't even going to go there. He will make it, got it?"

Rock shook his head and turned his back on them. Cookie led Callie over to the side of the clubhouse, and both of them leaned against the wall. She didn't know how long they stayed like that, but it felt like an eternity.

Finally the garage door opened, and Kink, Molly, and the doctor stepped out. They were covered in blood, and Cookie's pulse started beating frantically again. Callie took off toward her father, and he embraced her tightly. After several moments Callie finally let go, said something to Molly, and the other woman took her into the garage. Kink watched his daughter go, and this strange look covered his face. But he turned, held Cookie's gaze, and then smiled softly. She took off, not caring what anyone else said, and only acting on her instincts. She flew into his arms, crying for the first time in what felt like forever. She cried for Lucien who was hurt, cried because she was happy the other men were okay, and cried harder yet that Kink was holding her so tightly she could hardly breathe. It felt good to have him with her, felt good to let her anger, frustration, and most of all sadness leave her in this physical way.

"Baby, you doing okay?" Kink asked right beside her ear.

She nodded, knowing that her voice would be choked up. She closed her eyes, took a deep breath, and allowed herself to loosen her death grip on him. He was hesitant to let her go, and she smiled at that. "I'm okay. Are you and the other guys doing all right? Lucien is okay?" She hated asking, because she didn't know if she wanted to know the answer. She may have only been a part of the club for a few weeks, but they had kind of become her unofficial family.

He nodded and cupped her cheek. "I think, but I'll let the doctor go into that." He leaned down, kissed her hard and passionately, and then leaned back and rested his forehead on hers.

"You're trembling, Kink."

He nodded and kept his eyes closed. "I know, baby." He kissed her again, more softly this time, and moved her so she was positioned at his side. The other guys had moved forward, but they seemed to all be waiting for something.

The doctor cleared his throat and wiped his hand on a rag that one of the bikers had given him. The whiteness, or lack thereof, from the rag, startled her. There was so much blood.

So much.

"Lucien looks like he'll survive," the doctor said, and there was this collective sign that came from everyone. "The bullet was lodged in his thigh, but that is what saved his life. The bullet nicked his femoral artery, just barely, but if it had gone straight through he would have bled out."

"He needed blood?" Tuck asked. "I assume since it looked like he was bleeding a geyser back there." There was this uncomfortable silence that stretched between everyone.

"Yeah. I had Malcolm bring me the supplies I needed. Lucien's hooked up to a bag of type O negative, and although it is considered the universal donor blood type, there could be a rare reaction, and knowing the luck of the club lately that would be the case. I'm going to watch him closely for the next twenty-four hours."

"What the fuck does that mean about the blood?" Tuck asked with a bite of hostility in his voice.

"Easy, man. The doctor is doing all he can, okay?" Kink said. Right now they need to keep their heads together.

"Since I didn't know what his blood type is, type O negative is the best option." The doctor sighed heavily. "Listen, right now it's touch and go, but I'll stay with him for the next twenty-four hours. He's still unconscious, but his prognosis looks good right now." The doctor looked back at the garage and then glanced at the cabin. "I'm sorry, but that's all I have right now." The doctor looked at Kink. "I'm going to head inside and get a place set up downstairs for him."

"I'll go with you," Tuck said, and led the doctor inside.

"I should go check on Lucien again," Kink said, and gave Cookie a kiss on the forehead before turning. Cookie reached out and grabbed his forearm.

She glanced at the cabin, knowing Callie needed a little time in there. "Kink, come inside and let me help you get cleaned up." Even though neither of them said anything about it, Cookie could see the Kink knew she was referring to Callie being inside. "Just give her some time. She had some really bad news today."

God, she didn't want to be the one that said it, because after all that had happened that was the last thing they needed. But then again this news was big, and Callie needed to be the one to tell her father about her mom dying. Just as they went to go back inside Callie and Molly came out. Callie, surprisingly, wasn't in tears. "Go to her, Kink. Callie needs you right now."

Kink kissed her on the forehead, and went over to his daughter. He embraced her, but even from the distance Cookie could see that Callie was talking almost frantically. She waved her hands in fort of her and then burst into tears. Kink embraced her, stroked her hair, and Cookie's heart broke at the sight of such a strong, masculine man, looking over at her with this hollow expression in his eyes. She turned away, knowing that they didn't need an audience, and ushered the rest of the guys inside. "Come on, I think the girls were making something to eat." And right before she went inside she looked over her shoulder and saw one tear slide down Kink's cheek.

Chapter Fifteen

Five hours had passed since the guys had come back to the clubhouse. They had eaten breakfast in near silence, but then again Lucien was lying unconscious in the next room. He had gone through a pint of blood, and so far he hadn't had any negative reactions, which was a step in the right direction. No one knew how long he'd be out, but they were thankful he was alive. This life was screwed up in the worst kind of way, but then again they put themselves in this situation. It was in their blood, in their DNA.

Kink looked up at the loft, and although he couldn't see Callie or Cookie, he knew they were up there sleeping in one of the rooms. He sat at the bar, looking down at the shot Tatum had set in front of him. After Callie had told him about Sarah and Dale dying in that car accident he had called a buddy he knew on the force. Finding out the grisly details wasn't what Kink had been going for, but then he had found out they had both been drunk. That didn't make the situation any less horrendous, but it could have been even worse with other people being involved in the accident.

Fuck, what a shitty day. He took the shot and tossed it back. The alcohol burned, and it wasn't even noon yet, but he didn't care. He needed something to numb the pain, to take away the ugliness that surrounded him. It seeped into his life and was sucking the life right out of him.

The front door slammed opened, and Cain walked in, looking fierce, big, and pissed off. He scanned the room, stopped when he saw Kink, and moved swiftly over to him. "What the fuck happened, brother?" Cain was forty-five, but right now he looked old and tired, ready to kill someone, but most of all worried.

For the next twenty minutes Kink recapped on everything that happened, and then took him to see Lucien. The President was still unconscious, but his color wasn't so ashen anymore and his vitals were stable. They stayed in the room for another ten minutes before Cain finally needed a drink.

"That's fucked up, man," Cain said and sat at the bar. He asked for a shot from Tatum.

"You're finally out, man," Kink said. Although he was happy Cain was finally paroled, it was hard to be in a positive mood right now and celebrate.

"Yeah, but it fucking sucks coming here and seeing all this shit going down. I just wish I had been here to help out my brothers."

"Nah, I'm glad you didn't have to be in that situation. You've been locked up for a long damn time, and the last thing you needed was to be put in that situation."

Cain shook his head.

"But sorry about no welcome home party." Kink clapped him on the back. "But once things settle down and get back to normal, we'll party it up."

Cain stared down at his shot glass, and it was the same position as Kink had been in a few moments before. "Sounds good." Cain turned just his head and glanced at him. "I need to go see Fallina soon though."

Kink nodded. "How is she?" He hadn't planned on bringing up Cain's daughter, because although it had been a long time since everything had happened, and she was an adult now, that shit never left a father. Kink knew that if some fucker tried to mess with Callie, he'd kill them without even blinking.

"She's doing good, brother. She's working as a preschool teacher over in Chatham View. Doing good with her therapy and all that shit, so I can't complain."

This smile covered the big biker's face, and Kink couldn't help but feel the other man's fatherly love. Hell, it was what Kink felt for Callie. "She came up to see me every week during those nine years, man, and it broke my fucking heart to see her leave. But at the same time I didn't want her seeing me behind that glass."

Kink nodded and clapped Cain on the back again. "Take your time, and when you're ready, you know you'll always have a place at the table in River Run."

Cain nodded and tossed back the second shot Tatum put in front of him. "Thanks, Kink, but I have a lot of unfinished business to take care of, shit that might get me locked away for good this time." Cain looked at Kink, and the hardness in his black cold eyes spoke volumes. Cain wasn't nearly done with the asshole that hurt his daughter, and it was clear that the other man was going to get his revenge one way or another.

Kink leaned in close, and said, "If you need back-up, you know we are always here for you."

Cain nodded but didn't say anything. They sat in silence for a moment, and Kink realized he wanted to talk to Cain, to see how he was *really* doing. Prison changed a man, no matter how rough and tough he was. Cain might be a whopping six-foot-six, and even bigger in muscle mass now than when he went in, but once someone went to prison a little piece of him was chipped away for good. If Cain wanted to talk about it, then Kink and the rest of The Brothers would be here.

He wasn't going to get into what had happened to Sarah, not right now. There was so much heartache, anger, and mixed emotions that were swarming through the men right now. Bringing this up to Cain wouldn't do any good. There would be time to sit down, talk about everything, and make sure the information on both sides was out in the open. Several of the other members came forward and greeted Cain. They had all been friends for what seemed like a lifetime, and having the other man back was a good fucking thing, and would strengthen the club. "Listen, I'm going to talk to you later. I want to see my old lady."

Cain grinned. "I heard about that from the prospect that was jabber jaws in the car, Pierce, I think his name was."

Kink nodded. "Yeah, he likes to run his mouth."

"Old lady huh?" Cain asked, still smiling. "Never thought I'd see the day when your kinky ass would settle down. I'm happy for you."

Kink flipped Cain off good heartedly, but smiled. He turned and left Cain to talk with the other guys, and hunted out Cookie. He needed her, needed to hold her. There was nothing like a nightmare of a situation to put perspective on life in a man, even a stubborn, hardheaded bastard like him.

****

Lucien stared at Callie through the open doorway. He had woken up last night, was in some fucking pain, but thankful to be alive. He remembered everything up until he looked down at his thigh and saw the bullet wound. Then he had passed the hell out, and everything had been dark until last night. But the fucked-up part out of all of this, even after the gunfire, the dead bodies, and the bombing, was that Callie had been the first thing that came to his mind when consciousness took over. It was messed up in the worst kind of way, and although she wasn't quite eighteen yet, and he knew he would never touch her in that way because she was so young, he honestly didn't know if he'd be able to stay away when she was legal. It wasn't about a sexual relationship with her. It was a lot more complicated than that. He felt something in his cold heart when he looked at her, like it was beating solely for that one woman.

Fucking hell, Lucien.

He knew it was wrong to want her, knew it was against the unspoken code that no one in the club fucked with their kids. He didn't know why he had this need to be with her, to talk to her and make sure she was okay. It wasn't just about wanting to protect her because she was Kink's daughter, and that he would have done the same for any of the members' kids. It was a hell of a lot more, something that consumed him ever since he had seen her vulnerable at that bus stop with those assholes around her. He had been the one to help her, to make sure she was okay, and he knew there wasn't anything that could take that away, no matter how much he thought it should be gone.

All the Brothers had come to see him as soon as he had woken up, and that had gone a long way in helping him put Callie behind him, at least for those twenty minutes. But now she stepped into the room, and he felt his pain take a move to the back of his subconscious as the things he shouldn't feel moved through him. She looked tired and sad, and he wished like hell he could take that all away from her.

"Hi," she said softly, almost as if she were afraid to say anything.

"Hey, kid." He hadn't meant to call her that, because it almost seemed like a jab at their age difference. "You doing okay?"

She moved closer and pulled out a chair so that she was sitting beside his bed. "I'm okay," she said, and then stayed silent for a few seconds. "Listen, I don't know what to really say." She looked up from her lap, and this big tear slid down her cheek.

"Callie, what's wrong?"

She shook her head. "These are happy tears. I'm just glad you're okay. Seeing you lying there unconscious…" She swallowed roughly. "It was horrible, Lucien."

He shifted on the bed and gritted his teeth when pain lanced up his side.

"No, don't move. I just wanted to say I'm glad you're okay." She stood, but he reached out and took hold of her hand.

"Callie, I know when someone is lying to me. Tell me what the fuck is wrong."

She stared at him for a moment and slowly pulled her hand away. She curled her fingers into her palm so they formed tight fists on her thighs. "My life feels like it's unraveling right before me, like I can't control anything anymore." She was crying steadily now and lifted her hand to brush the tears away. "My mom died, Lucien. Her and Dale were in a car accident the other day—"

He didn't say anything, didn't know what to say that would make the situation any less horrific. He stopped her from continuing by pulling her closer and wrapping his arms around her body. The pain was excruciating, but holding her, having her close to him, made that discomfort feel like an annoyance. She shook and cried, and all he could do was hold her. For the first time in his fucking life, he felt at a loss on how to control a situation, he and didn't know how to make it right.

Chapter Sixteen

Two weeks later

Cookie tightened her hold on Kink's waist and rested her cheek against his back. His cut was smooth leather and buttery soft, and the smell of age and of it being well cared for filled her nose. She closed her eyes and couldn't stop herself from smiling. Two weeks had already passed, and although that really wasn't any time at all, it still felt like years had already gone by. Although it had been a couple of weeks since Kink and the other guys had come back from dealing with the cult, and things were slowly starting to get back to the way they had been, there was still this heaviness that was with all of the guys. Cookie could feel it weighing down on the club, and when she was around the guys it felt suffocating. That part of the danger might be over with, but there was still the death of Callie's mom, Lucien almost dying, and something else going on that she couldn't figure out yet.

Lucien was on the mend, but he seemed different, more reserved. Maybe that was the weirdness that she also felt, like he was holding something back? After he got shot he certainly was harder now, if that was even possible, and the look in his eyes was always calculating. It was different from how it was before. She didn't know him very well, but even then she knew he was a powerful man. Now he seemed almost dead inside, and although she didn't know how to help him, she wanted to regardless. But then again it really wasn't her place to try to help anyone that wasn't ready to be helped, and whatever Lucien was going through was something he wasn't ready to let go of just yet.

Over the last two weeks her relationship with Kink had progressed slowly, but she was thankful for that. When she had first started working for the club she had only seen herself traveling the country and not settling in one spot. Although she still wanted to do that, she also saw herself here, in River Run, and in Kink and even Callie's life. She had never had anyone in her life that really mattered, and certainly hadn't ever had anyone that cared for her in a genuine way. But she had that here, with the MC. It warmed her, made her feel like she wasn't a waste of space, and wasn't that what life was all about? Now she sat on the back of his Harley with the wind blowing through her hair, the sun streaming down on her back, and the strength and power she felt from Kink filling her. The thought of Callie consumed her for a moment, and she wanted to cry for the young girl all over again. It might have only been fourteen days since Callie had found out about her mom passing, but the girl was strong, and she was taking one day at a time. She was moving on with her life and trying not letting the grief consume her. But Cookie was there for her, and so was Kink. Cookie may only be a few years older than Callie, but she cared about her, and saw her as this vulnerable and damaged young woman who needed to know she was loved. Callie needed to know she wasn't alone, and that Cookie knew how she felt, knew the desperation that could consume a person until there was nothing left. With Callie's eighteenth birthday only a couple of weeks away, Cookie had been trying to make this a memorable celebration. Cookie didn't want a celebration that would further bring sadness to her life since this would be the first birthday Callie would have to celebrate without her mother here.

The funeral had passed, a hard situation, but surprisingly Callie had asked Cookie to go with her. They had been getting closer ever since Callie had gotten the phone call, and she couldn't help but see herself in Callie. And then Cookie had helped Callie move out of her mother's house and in with Kink. Cookie might not live with Kink, despite how much she cared about him, but she knew that right now he needed to be there for Callie. It was going to be a long road for her, and right now she needed to be surrounded by people that cared for her.

They had been riding for the last twenty minutes, and were well outside of River Run city limits. Cookie pushed all of the grief and sorrow that had filled her life in the past, and when she had been with the club, and rested her hands behind her. She may not be holding onto Kink any further, but this small bit of freedom made her feel like the world wasn't as grim as she had always seen it. With her eyes closed she tilted her head back and breathed in deeply. Being like this felt as if she were flying, as if nothing tethered her to the world and she could just float away without any worries.

"You doing good, baby?" Kink asked over the rumble of the Harley's engine.

"Yeah," she said, and heard the happiness, excitement, and even relief in her voice. They were going to the small lake that sat between River Run and Steel Corner. She had read up about the sights around the town when she had first been brought to River Run, but had stayed in this little bubble of her life. The lake was a secluded area that was mainly used for fishing and boating, but the spot Kink said they were going to was more isolated and private. This spot was quiet and the perfect place for them to spend some time together. She wasn't about to talk about her former life, about her past or what had happened to her again. That was done, she had said what she needed to say, and she hoped Kink respected that. She just wanted to move on now.

He drove his bike down the gravel road for another five minutes and finally pulled off to the side and cut the engine. He was off the Harley first, and had his hands wrapped around her waist and hauled her off the bike before she could even move. For several seconds all Kink did was hold her, and she knew he was still dealing with the almost death of a man he considered a part of his family. It had been hard for all the members, but it seemed like Kink was taking it especially hard. She knew Lucien was like a brother to Kink, and although she comforted him, until she had actually started to care about the people that surrounded her, she hadn't been able to relate to the bombardment of emotion. But she also knew the club members held themselves in check. Cookie could see on their faces the anger that they barely restrained. These men weren't just bikers or alpha all the way—they were a breed all their own.

The sound of the wind whistling through the trees had a hypnotic quality to it, but it was the sound of Kink's beating heart beneath her ear that lulled her to calmness. He grabbed a blanket from one of his saddlebags and reached out to take her hand. Kink led them down the path that led to the lake, and then laid the blanket out in front of the water. Kink gestured for her to have a seat. They sat side-by-side, neither saying anything, and both focusing on the water.

He turned and faced her after a few moments, and just stared at her. Then he lifted his other hand and cupped her cheek. "I have a lot of things on my mind, Cookie, things that make me realize that I don't want to spend my life without you, baby."

"I feel the same way, Kink."

He shook his head slowly. "No, baby, I don't think you realize how much I care about you." He took her hand and placed it right over his heart. The act was so very gentle and caring that it brought a wave of emotion to her. This biker was big, muscular, and brought fear in other men with just a look. But here he was, holding her hand over his heart, and looking at her with this vulnerable, open expression. "I've already talked to you about being my old lady, but I want you to know it means more than just being there, Cookie." He started rubbing his thumb along her cheek with his other hand, and she lifted her hand and placed it over his. It was strange to be able to feel someone's emotions as strongly as if they were her own.

"I know this is going to sound fucking crazy, but, Cookie, baby, you're my life." He let go of her and faced the lake once more. It seemed like ages that they sat there in silence, but it was a very comfortable, easy silence.

"The shit I've seen and done sometimes keeps me up at night, Cookie." He faced her again. "But since you've come into my life I've realized that all the dark shit I've done doesn't compare to the pure feeling I have for you."

For the next fifteen minutes she listened to him talk about Callie and everything he had been through with Sarah. She didn't speak, just listened to him unload this burden that clearly weighed heavily on him.

"I know you talked a little about your past, but I want you to know that I'm here to listen to whatever you have to say."

She smiled and glanced down at his lips. "Honestly, talking about all the bad stuff that happened while I was growing up doesn't change anything, and it doesn't help me in some kind of therapeutic way." She searched his face with her gaze. "It isn't that I don't trust you, or don't want to confide in you—"

"I get it." He smiled softly. "I really do understand, and I'm okay with whatever you decide. I know that rehashing all that toxic stuff doesn't help some people." He leaned in and pressed his forehead to hers. "I just want you to know that if you ever need someone to talk to, I hope you let me be that person you need."

They had already started rebuilding the MC building that had gotten bombed. The girls had moved out of the clubhouse and back to the cabin since the explosion hadn't affected it. It had been nice staying at the clubhouse, being around the guys while Lucien recovered, and spending time with Callie. She had learned a lot about the young girl in these last couple of weeks, and not just the pain that Callie felt. Cookie hadn't spoken to her about Lucien, although she wanted to, because she could see how Callie looked at the club President. It was the same longing way Lucien looked at Callie. That was going to be another situation that stirred shit up, for sure, especially if Lucien and Callie acted on what they felt for each other. But fortunately Kink was so focused on Callie's feelings with the passing of Sarah that he wasn't even paying attention to the chemistry happening with his daughter and the much older Lucien. He was blind to a lot of things, stuff that would most likely put him in a rage if he ever realized what was happening right in front of him. Cookie had thought about bringing it up to Kink, but she realized it wasn't her place. She didn't know for sure what was going on, and Callie needed to bring this up.

She pressed her lips to his, closed her eyes, and then moved off of him. He looked surprised at first, but when she started removing her clothing the heat started to cover his expression. When she was naked in front of him she held her hand out. It took him only a couple of seconds to take what she offered, and then he was getting undressed, too. Cookie didn't even care if someone saw them, didn't care if what they were doing was standing naked in a public place. All she wanted was to have some solace with the man she was falling for. With his hand in hers, she didn't say anything as she led them to the water's edge. The temperature around them was warm with a slight breeze, but the water was frigid when she stepped into it.

"Skinny dipping?" he asked with amusement in his voice.

She didn't respond, just smiled as she looked over her shoulder, and continued to lead him into the water. "God, this is so cold."

"I can warm you up," he said right beside her ear, and then in the next instant he had his arms wrapped around her waist and they were both crashing into the water. She went under the water, but Kink had her out of the water a second later, and pressed to the hardness of his chest.

She gasped out and wiped the water away from her face. "Shit." She cried out, and goose-bumps popped out along her flesh.

Kink nuzzled her neck, and his warm breath helped heat up her cold body. He moved them further into the water, and she grew used to the temperature. "I told you I could warm you up," he said against the side of her throat, and she grinned. They were still touching the ground, but she had her arms wrapped tightly around him and her head resting on his chest.

"I trust you Kink, and I know you'd listen to anything that I told you," she said softly, and inhaled deeply. "I just want to start over with you." She pulled back and looked up at him. Kink only stared at her for a few seconds before he leaned down and claimed her mouth. For long, drugging minutes all they did was kiss. She felt how hard he was against her belly, and a wave of arousal slammed into her, stealing her breath and making her want him with desperation. But before she could tell him that he had her in his arms and out of the water.

He was about to lay her on her back, but Cookie shifted so that she was straddling his waist, and cupped his face with her hands. Maybe sex wasn't what they needed right now, but it was the most powerful way to express how someone felt.

"I love you, baby, and I have never told another woman that, never wanted to kill for a woman, or devote my life to one the way I want to do with you." He stared into her eyes, breathed in deeply, and exhaled just as forcefully.

Water dripped off of both of them, and she ran her hands through his hair. "I want so much with you, Kink."

He kissed her again, and again, and when she went to reach between their bodies he stopped her and pulled back. "Being my old lady means that I'll protect you with my life, *give* you my life, Cookie." He kissed her again, and the desire to be with him, to show him how much he meant to her rose swiftly inside of her. "I've claimed you already, baby, devoted myself to you because you *are* my world now. You, Callie, and this club." He stared at her hard. "That is all I have left, and I'm not about to let you go."

She held each side of his face, too, and stared into his eyes just as fiercely as he was watching her. "I love you, too, Kink." The stubble on his cheeks was rough against her palms.

The sharp slashes of his eyebrows over his bright blue eyes were as masculine as they were beautiful. He had one of those strong noses, a set of full lips, and a square jaw. On the outside he was the epitome of what she thought a man should look like: powerfully built, dangerous, and protective. But she could see the *real* Logan "Kink" Roberts. "There is so much more to you,

Kink, so much that you hide." Water droplets fell from his dark hair, slid down his face, and dropped down to his hard, defined chest.

"I'm not hiding, baby. I'm right here, out in the open for you to see, baring my fucking soul," he murmured against her lips. "You deserve a man better than me, but I'll spend the rest of my life proving that I can be worthy of you."

She wanted to knock some sense into him, to tell him that he was worthy of everything he wanted. Cookie had never been the take charge kind of person, but for some reason she felt so much stronger being with Kink. "My entire life people have been putting me down, telling me that I wasn't worth shit."

A low, dangerous sound left him, and he wrapped his arms around her tightly. "Baby, you are worth so fucking much—"

She cupped his cheeks again and leaned down to kiss him lightly. "I'm done talking about the bad stuff, Kink. I want to focus on us, on Callie, and making it through all of this."

"I'll say it over and over again, because it will always be true." He leaned in and this time was the one to kiss her. "I am not good enough for you, but I swear to fucking God that I will spend the rest of my life showing you that you are mine, baby." He took her mouth again, not softly, but full of possession and need, matching her own. "Come over tight for dinner. Let me show you that being with me won't always be about the violence and drama."

She pulled back and grinned. "You want to cook for me?"

When he winked her heart picked up speed.

"I'm not saying I'm Gordon Ramsey or anything, but I think I can rustle something edible up." His face took on a somber expression. "Besides, I think Callie would love to have you over."

"Okay," she said softly. "I'd love to come over."

He kissed her again, and soon that soft, gentle kiss turned frantic as they pressed their tongues together, moved them around in a sexual manner, and repeated the action over and over again. Her pulse raced, and her pussy became wet. All it took to get her so aroused she couldn't think straight was a kiss from Kink. She could feel how rock hard he was. It was like a lead pipe between her thighs, creating even more wetness and having her clit swell from her desire. But that kiss and his clenching fingers on her hips started to take on a faster, more demanding pace. She was just as needy as he was.

For a second all she did was look at his chest and run her hands over the smooth, tattooed and hairless skin that covered him. Cookie never thought she'd be one that grew aroused with tattooed skin, especially for as many tattoos as Kink had, but she was aroused, and growing more so just looking at him. The collage of ink spanned over his pecs, down his abdomen, and around his waist. Some were colorful, and others black and white, but they all were bold, vibrant, and powerfully drawn. He even had some ink that moved up his chest and over his neck.

"You keep looking at me like that, Bailey, and I'm going to fucking devour you."

More moisture left her when he cupped her breasts, squeezed the mounds rhythmically, and leaned in to suck her left nipple into his mouth. God, she loved when he said her real name. He made this deep rooted noise in the back of his throat. For long drugging moments he bit and sucked at the turgid peak, and then alternated to her other side. The blood rushed to the surface as he tormented and teased her, and soon she was grasping the short strands of his hair and moaning out for more. She didn't care if anyone could see. All she wanted was Kink, right here and now, and for them to put everything behind them and only focus on each other.

"I am so fucking hard for you, baby." He murmured the words against her breasts but didn't stop sucking on her flesh. "Can you feel it?" He lifted his hips slightly so his cock rubbed along her folds. Cookie let her head fall back and closed her eyes. It felt so good having his warm, wet mouth on her body that all Cookie could think about was having Kink throw her on the ground and slide this hard, thick length right up inside of her.

"Take me, Kink. Fuck me right here." She might have lived a gritty life, but she had never outright asked someone to fuck her. But Kink was different, and this life she was now living was different. In a move so quick she didn't even realize what was happening he was standing with her in his arms. He turned around and had her on her back on the blanket with his huge body over hers. He placed his hands on her inner thighs, wrenched them open, and stared at her pussy like he was starving and ready to devour her alive.

"You're so fucking wet for me, Cookie."

All she could do was lie there and let him look his fill. But she liked the way he watched her with hungry eyes. She gripped his broad shoulders and pulled him closer to her. They kissed again and again and once more until she was lifting her hips, and seeking his hardness. His hands were everywhere on her, touching her pussy, rubbing her slick, bare folds until she was muttering unintelligible words. She then felt the hot length of his cock press against her inner thigh. The slickness of his pre-cum at the tip of his shaft moved along her heated flesh. They kissed again and moved their tongues together. With his mouth still on hers, he reached between their bodies and placed his cock against her slick folds.

He rubbed the length up and down her cleft. She thought he'd plunge in deep, claim her like he had before, and make her forget about everything except what was happening right now. But what he did next surprised the hell out of her.

He had her on her belly, and positioned her so that her lower body was off the ground. Kink had his hands on the mounds of her ass before she could even blink. All she felt was the warm breath of Kink moving closer to her body. His body heat and the harsh puffs of air that came from him bathed her ass and pussy, and had her closing her eyes as the delicious sensations moved through her.

"Fuck, baby, the things I want to do to you." He palmed her ass. "The dirty, hard and rough things that would make you scream out my name as you come so hard you couldn't even hold yourself up anymore."

She curled her fingers into the blanket.

"But we have all the time in the world to show to you the darker side of pleasure, the ones where I give you so much of it that you gasp out my name and beg me to never stop."

A stinging pain covered on her ass cheeks, and Cookie snapped her eyes open at the same time Kink spanked her other cheek. He did this repeatedly, alternated between the mounds of her bottom until the blood rushed to the surface and her skin heated. It wasn't painful, but more stimulating than anything else, and had her soaked even more.

"Is that good, baby?" He stopped spanking her and spread her ass as open as it would go until the air touched her anus. He clenched and released her flesh in a way that stimulated and eased her.

"Yes," she breathed out.

She felt him place his finger at the entrance of her pussy and rub the digit around the hole. She parted her lips and closed her eyes again as he ran his thumb along her entrance, and moved her wetness up her cleft and rubbing it along her clit. He slid the finger back down to her pussy hole, and gently teased her, probed it a little, and had her on the verge of screaming for more.

"I need you," Kink said, and in the next second was on his back and had her hauled on top of him so she straddled his waist again.

She looked down at him, saw the strain of his muscles right below his tatted up skin, and pressed her pelvis down. Cookie ground herself unabashedly against him, smeared her wetness along his lower belly and his cock, and moaned out at how good it felt.

"That's it, baby, work that wet cunt all over me." He held onto her hips tightly. "Take my cock, Cookie, and put it in your tight little pussy."

She panted and rose up on her knees, took the root of his dick in her hand, and squeezed him until he hissed out and curled his fingers even harder into her skin. She was so wet her cream slipped from her. She could see that Kink was watching that trail with heated approval.

"Do it, baby, slide my big fucking cock all the way up inside of you." His chest rose and fell hard. "Don't torture me. I'm barely hanging on as it is."

She placed the head of his erection at her entrance and stated to push down.

"I swear we will do the soft and sweet kind of sex that I want to give you, but right now I need it this way, baby," he ground out.

Cookie liked having sex this way with him, this raw and untamed kind. It was full of real emotion, and that was exactly what she needed. There was the ever-present stretching and burning sensation as the girth of his cockhead parted her opening. Before she was even halfway down he lifted his hips up, shoving the rest of his shaft inside of her.

"Yeah, baby. *Christ*, Cookie, you are so tight and wet." His voice was this deep, serrated sound, like a sharpened knife moving along her body. And then she was the one taking control of the movements. She placed her hands on his chest, took only a second to trace the outline of his MC patch logo tattoo on his pec, and then lifted her hips and shoved herself back down on him. He groaned; she gasped in pleasure, and she repeated the action repeatedly. Her breasts shook forcefully as she bounced up and down on him and felt her pussy grow pliant and impossibly wetter. It was like another entity filled her as she moved up and down on top of Kink.

"Come on, baby. Come so fucking hard for me," Kink roared out.

She felt his cock swell inside of her, felt the first powerful jet of his release fill her, warm her and cause another round of aftershocks to move through her veins. "It's so good." The words tumbled from her. Kink didn't verbally respond, just grunted out and continued to fill her with his cum. He rose up while she was still moving on top of him, and wrapped his arms around her. When the ecstasy faded, she sagged against him, not able to hold herself up anymore.

"You're mine, Cookie," Kink said softly. "And I'm not letting you go."

"I don't want you to let me go." And she meant that with every part of her body.

****

Cookie sat around the small kitchen table with Kink on one side and Callie on the other. Molly had dropped her off about an hour ago, and it was when she walked through the front door and saw them standing there, that she felt like she was accepted and actually part of something more. They had finished eating a little bit ago, and the comfortable, warm silence that moved among them had her smiling.

"Callie, have you been putting anymore applications in?" Cookie asked, trying to bring the conversation to something that the young woman might look forward to. Although she put on a brave front, there were times when Callie looked like she had broken everything inside of her, and didn't know how to put the pieces back.

She shrugged. "A few, but honestly I haven't been giving college much thought. I don't know if I want to go or not."

"What?" Kink asked and lifted his bottle of beer to his mouth. He was staring at his daughter as he drank, and the frustration on his face was clear.

"Kink," Cookie said softly, and when he finally looked at her she gave him this hard expression that meant, "don't push." Cookie understood that he wanted what was best for Callie, but despite the problems Callie had with her mother she had still lost the person who had given birth to her.

"No, it's okay, Cookie." Callie looked at Kink. "I don't know if I want to go to college right now, Dad. I know I do some day, but I don't know if right after graduation is the step I want to take."

Kink swallowed loudly, set his beer down, and then exhaled. "I know. I just don't want you to hold yourself back."

Callie shook her head, grabbed her plate, and then stood. "Dad, just please. I have so much on my plate now. Graduation, college, Mom dying, and…" She was the one to swallow now, and when she looked between Kink and Cookie, there was this strange almost detachment and sadness that covered her face. "Just please." And then she turned and left, and Cookie knew that she was going to cry.

"I should go talk to her, tell her I didn't mean to seem like I'm pushing," Kink said and went to stand, but Cookie reached out and placed her hand on his.

"Kink, just let her go this one time. She's dealing with stuff, and sometimes people just need to grieve by themselves." She smiled and ran her fingers over his warm skin.

Kink rested back on his chair and looked over at the stairs where Callie had ascended. "I feel like I wasn't really there for her," he said but still stared at the stairs. "I left her with Sarah, because I thought that was the best option for her." He looked at Cookie. "But it wasn't, and now Sarah is gone. Callie is suffering through this, and so much more, and I feel like I'm lost."

"She's a teenager that just lost a woman that she might not have gotten along with, but that she called 'Mom'. She's the only mother she had, and now that Sarah is gone, you're what she has. Give her time, and she'll come around." Cookie didn't know anything about families and what should and shouldn't happen in them. She didn't have that kind of family life growing up, but what she did know was that even when someone had a support system and people that loved them solitude was sometimes the best option for them.

The sound of Callie coming back down the stairs had them both looking in her direction. She stopped in the dining room with her coat on and her purse slung over her bag. "Do you care if I head out for a few hours?"

"Where are you going?" Kink asked.

"Honestly? Nowhere. I just want to drive around and clear my head. Maybe I'll meet up with Ian for some coffee or a movie. I don't know." Callie seemed tired, but not n the exhausted, needing sleep kind of way.

Cookie squeezed his hand again, and he breathed out.

"Be home by midnight, okay?" he said as if it took a lot to let her leave. When Callie walked over to him and hugged him, there was this moment where all they did was hold each other.

"I love you, Dad." Callie pulled away, and Kink pushed a piece f her hair behind her ear.

"I love you, too, and please be careful."

Callie nodded.

"And please, if you plan on getting drunk give me a call and I'll come pick you up."

For a second Callie just stood there, her cheeks turning red, and her eyes widening slightly.

"You okay?" Kink asked her.

She licked her lips and nodded. "I'm fine." She lifted her hand and waved at Cookie. "Bye." When the front door shut behind her Cookie exhaled and held Kink's hand again.

"She'll come to you when she'd ready." She squeezed his hand.

He nodded.

"How about getting me something strong to drink?" Cookie said.

Kink looked at her and smiled. "If you get drunk I am going to make you stay here for the night."

She leaned forward and said, "I was planning on it anyway." She wanted to be here for Kink, but she also wanted to be here for Callie. How strange, but wonderful, that in such a short time frame she could come to care about these two people so damn much.

Chapter Seventeen

One week later

Kink, Malice, and Lucien all sat around the card table, beers in front of them and a pile of cash in the center of the table. Lucien was still recovering, and staying at the club where everyone could look after him and help him if he needed anything seemed like the best thing. Right now the club was quiet, with most of the guys out for the evening, either at their places, getting drunk at one of the local bars, or even watching over the girls at the cabin. Cookie was at home, going over online classes she wanted to take in the fall. Kink was proud of her for taking that step, and glad that she was finishing something to help keep her busy. Although he didn't want to tell her what to do or keep her locked up because he wanted to keep her safe, this was her life, and she had had enough people holding her back. Because she was thinking about going to school she was working less at the club, and honestly he was thankful for that. No fucking way did he want his old lady here seeing all the raunchy shit these guys did.

"I'll raise ten," Malice said and tossed the money in the center.

"I fold," Lucien said and tossed his cards down. "How's Adrianna doing?" Lucien asked.

Malice leaned back and grinned. "She's good, real good actually." Malice tossed his cards down, face-up, and his grin widened. "She actually kicked me out of the house so her and Dakota can have a movie, popcorn, and pizza date."

Kink started chuckling. "It takes a strong woman to handle your ass, Malice."

Lucien started laughing, and then groaned.

"Easy, sir-laugh-a-lot," Malice said, and Kink burst out laughing.

"You got one strong woman, too, Kink," Lucien said, and reached out for his beer. He tossed the rest of the alcohol back.

The front doors burst open, and they turned and stared at Cain. But Cain wasn't alone, and the man that he dragged in, half dead, busted and bruised, and spilling blood on the club floor.

They stood in unison, looked at each other, and then looked at Cain again.

"Brother, what the fuck is going on?" Lucien asked, but Kink already knew what was happening.

Cain lifted the groaning man high enough that they got a look at his fucked-up face, and then he tossed him onto the floor. The guy's head cracked against the ground, and Cain walked over his body. From the distance Kink could see the busted up knuckles Cain was sporting as he reached across the bar for a bottle of tequila. He drank a good portion of it before slamming the bottle back on the bar, and then turned around and faced them. "That motherfucker right there." He tipped his chin toward the guy on the ground.

"Is the one that messed with Fallina." Kink finished Cain's sentence, and the other club member nodded.

"What the hell are you doing bringing him here?" Malice asked and moved over to the guy, pushed him onto his back with a boot, and stared down at him.

"I am kind of low on places I can torture a prick that tried to rape my daughter," Cain said and looked at Lucien. "I need a place to store him until I'm done."

"Done doing what?" Kink pretty much knew what Cain wanted to do, and he didn't blame the man. If it was reversed and some asshole had tried touching his kid he would have torn their limbs off and sat there to watch them die.

"Getting vengeance for all the pain my daughter has had to live with because of this bastard." Cain grabbed the bottle again and drank more, his stare trained on the man on the floor.

The three of them moved over to Cain, stared at the man who was like their family, and watched as the emotions played across his face.

"I want to watch him hurt, want to see the pain on his face, and want to have him realize that he'll die at my hands., Cain gritted out. "And I didn't know where else to go, so once I found out where the asshole was, this was the first place I thought of."

Lucien grabbed his shoulder, and Kink could see him squeezing it lightly. "He hurt your daughter, and that means he messed with this whole fucking club." Lucien moved a step back. "Let's take him to the garage. The cement floor is coated so the blood won't stain."

And then they were hauling the man out that was about to live the last moments of his life out in agony.

The End

www.jenikasnow.com

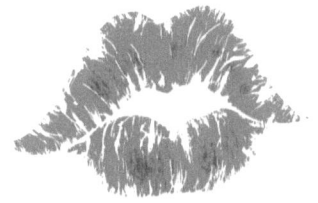

EVERNIGHT PUBLISHING ®

www.evernightpublishing.com